THE
DAWN
OF
LOVE

Barbara Cartland

THE
DAWN
OF
LOVE

E. P. Dutton • New York

For information contact:
E.P. Dutton, 2 Park Avenue,
New York, N.Y. 10016

Library of Congress Cataloging in Publication Data:
Cartland, Barbara, 1902-
The dawn of love

I. Title.
PZ3.C247Daw 1980 [PR6005.A765] 823'.9'12 79-14992
ISBN: 0-525-08890-3
Published simultaneously in Canada by
Clarke, Irwin & Company
Limited, Toronto and Vancouver

10 9 8 7 6 5 4 3 2 1

First Edition

Author's Note

George Bernard Shaw published his play *Pygmalion* in 1913. This story of a flower-girl trained by a phonetician to pass as a lady, although a most effective satire upon the English class-system, is less a play of ideas than are Shaw's other major plays.

Its rich human content made it a favourite with the public both as a Musical on the Stage and on the screen with Rex Harrison and Audrey Hepburn in the leading parts.

Cecil Beaton's exquisite decor and dresses contributed to its success, and Eliza Doolittle is one of Shaw's unforgettable personalities.

Chapter One

1913

The Honourable Peregrine Gillingham jumped out of the hansom, paid the cabby, and walked up the steps of Windlemere House.

The front door was already open, and he handed his tall hat to a footman who wore a powdered wig, then nodded to the Butler.

"Good-evening, Dawkins!"

"Good-evening, Sir."

"Is His Grace in the Library?"

"Yes, Sir, he's been waiting for nearly an hour."

There was a touch of rebuke in the Butler's well-modulated voice, and Peregrine smiled to himself as he followed the servant's rather pompous tread across the marble Hall.

Windlemere House, of all the magnificent mansions in Park Lane, was the most outstanding.

It had been built by the Duke's grandfather and was the Early Victorians' idea of what a Ducal house should look like.

Fortunately, there was still an architectural hangover from the Georgian period, so it had been designed in better taste than had many of its neighbours.

But Peregrine was not concerned with Windlemere House, which he had seen often enough. He was only hoping that Alstone would not be in one of his disagreeable moods because he was late.

The Duke had an awe-inspiring affect on friend and foe alike, and even Peregrine, who was one of his closest friends, found that when he withdrew into an icy reserve to show his disapproval, it was distinctly depressing.

"Mr. Peregrine Gillingham, Your Grace!" Dawkins announced at the Library-door, and the Duke, who was reading *The Times,* looked up from the newspaper to say:

"Perry! Why the devil are you so late?"

"I'm sorry, Alstone," his friend replied, advancing towards him. "My father sent for me unexpectedly, and you know how long-winded he is."

The Duke threw down the paper to say:

"I suppose I must accept that as an excuse, as I well know that there's no stopping your father once he gets going on a subject that interests him."

"He was not particularly interested," Perry replied ruefully, "only annoyed."

"Money?" the Duke questioned.

"Of course. What else does my father ever talk to me about?"

"You should not be so extravagant!"

"That's all very well for you . . ." Perry began; then realising that the Duke was teasing him, he laughed.

"All right, I have been slightly overdoing it lately, but you know as well as I do that Molly is extremely expensive, and very much more so since you took an interest in her."

"I did not 'spoil the market,' as you so often tell me I do, for long," the Duke replied.

"Long enough," Perry said. "You gave her a taste not only for caviare and champagne, but for diamonds, and my allowance from my father has never been able to stretch that far."

He groaned before he added:

"It's hell being a younger son—a situation you have never had to face."

"I also have my difficulties," the Duke replied.

"It bewilders me to think what they can possibly be," Perry replied.

As he spoke, he accepted a glass of champagne from a silver tray presented to him by a footman.

The Duke also took a glass, and then the bottle of champagne, which Dawkins carried, was placed in a magnificent silver wine-cooler filled with ice before the two servants withdrew.

"You were telling me about your troubles," the Duke said with a faint smile. "Would you like to listen to mine?"

"I would be delighted, but I've always imagined you had none."

"Mine are not financial but mental," the Duke replied. "The truth is, Perry, I was thinking before you arrived that I am bored!"

Peregrine sat upright.

"My God! Alstone," he said, "if ever I heard a preposterous statement, that is the tallest! You, bored? You, who have everything? I do not believe it!"

"It is true," the Duke answered, "and I blame you because by being late you have made me realise it."

"What in God's name have you to be bored

about?" Perry asked. "You are the richest man in the British Isles and the biggest land-owner, you own the finest and most outstanding horses, and you have the pick of every 'Fair Charmer' who takes your fancy!"

He drew in his breath before he continued:

"And we all know the answer to that—it's because you are so damned good-looking, the hero of any maiden's dreams!"

"Shut up, Perry, you make me feel sick!" the Duke interposed.

"It's nothing to what you make me feel by saying you are bored! Shall I go on with a list of the rest of your possessions? Your yacht, your Château in France with the best boar-hunting in Europe, your salmon river . . ."

"Keep quiet!" the Duke ordered. "What I am talking about is something quite different."

"In what way?"

"I think I can best express it as a need for mental stimulation," the Duke said slowly. "The trouble is that everything I do has a certain familiarity about it which completely eliminates any element of surprise or of anticipation."

He was speaking surprisingly seriously and his friend looked at him in perplexity.

Perry was in fact quite intelligent when he wanted to be. He realised now that the Duke was not joking or speaking idly, but clearly pursuing an unusual and serious train of thought.

"I was thinking last night when we were playing poker," the Duke went on, "that we all knew one another too well for the game to be really amusing. I know immediately when Archie has a good hand because his eyes flicker, Charles's lips tighten when he has a bad one, and you click your fingers when you draw to a straight flush!"

"Dammit all, Alstone, that's almost cheating!" Perry protested.

"On the contrary, it's simply being observant, and thus knowing for sure what is going to happen—which, I may add, applies also to my other interests."

"I suppose by that you are referring to Daisy," Perry hazarded. "I have felt for some time that she was beginning to get on your nerves."

He thought for a moment that he had gone too far. The Duke was always very reserved when it came to anybody speaking of his love-affairs.

But tonight he was in a confiding mood.

"Daisy is without exception the most beautiful woman in London," he said, "but even beauty can have a certain sameness about it."

"I agree," Perry replied.

He thought, as he spoke, that he was not surprised that the Duke was growing bored with the Countess of Hellingford.

There was no doubt about her beauty, which was breath-taking when you first saw it, but she was also inclined to be possessive and at times bossy, and, to be honest, he was surprised that the Duke had tolerated her for as long as he had.

"What about a trip abroad?" he said aloud.

"Where shall I go?" the Duke enquired. "Another thing I was considering last night was that I have visited nearly all the most attractive places in the world, so unless I am prepared to cross the Gobi Desert or climb Mount Everest, there is not much left for me to do."

Perry laughed.

"It really is a case of 'poor little rich boy'!"

"Exactly!" the Duke agreed disarmingly. "And so I am asking you for suggestions."

"For goodness' sake, confine your enquiries to me," Perry said. "You know what a furore it would cause if you said anything like this to The Gang. They are very content with things as they are."

The Duke's lips curved in a cynical smile.

He was well aware that what Perry called The Gang was a collection of his friends who depended on him for their racing, fishing, yachting, shooting, and every other entertainment which was provided so generously on the Duke's Estates and in the many houses he possessed.

It had become almost a habit for him to entertain the same people every weekend at Mere, his large and extremely fine house in Surrey.

His special coterie of friends looked on it so much as part of their existence that the same bedrooms were always kept ready for them, and they even left a number of their personal possessions behind to save the bother of taking them back to London.

If the Duke intended to change his way of life, Perry thought, there would certainly be weeping and wailing amongst what he secretly called "hangers-on," and he had no wish to be there to listen to it.

"Where are you thinking of going?" he asked.

"I'm not going anywhere, as far as I know," the Duke replied. "I am just asking you what I should do, what I might find interesting, instead of sitting waiting as I am now and feeling as if I am becoming fossilised."

"That is the last thing you will ever be!" Perry exclaimed. "At the same time, I understand what you are saying to me, and I shall try to think of a solution."

"All I want is something new; something which is different from the ordinary pattern which makes my life at the moment seem as dull and unruffled as a duck-pond."

"Would you change places with me?" Perry asked. "I can assure you there would be a great deal of ruffle if you had to listen to my father croaking on about responsibility, extravagance, and my aimless life which shows that I am nothing but a waster!"

The Duke laughed.

"Your father has always resented your being a friend of mine. He does not think I take my responsibilities seriously enough, as he told my father almost before I was old enough to wear long trousers."

"If he could hear you at the moment," Perry said, "he would realise that you are taking everything far too seriously. Enjoy yourself, Alstone! Or why not try marriage? That would certainly be a change!"

There was, for a moment, an ominous silence. Then the Duke said:

"You know the answer to that. Never again! Never!"

"That is the most ridiculous statement you have ever made!" Perry said. "Of course you have to marry sometime. What about an heir?"

"My brother Thomas has three sons."

"That is not the same as having one yourself. It would amuse you to teach your own boy to ride and shoot, and to know that he would carry on the family traditions."

"It is a picture that does not appeal to me in the slightest," the Duke said firmly. "When Elaine was killed I had no feeling of grief, and I can assure you that having escaped the noose of matrimony once, I have no wish to put the rope round my neck for a second time."

Perry did not answer.

He was remembering that the Duke had been very young when his father arranged for him to marry the daughter of another Duke.

From a social point of view it had been an admirable alliance, but the bride and bridegroom had quarrelled from the moment they had left the Church, and when Alstone's wife was killed while out hunting, everyone expected him to marry again.

From that moment, however, he made it clear that his intentions where women were concerned were strictly dishonourable.

Surrounded and pursued by the loveliest and most sophisticated women in Society, he chose to amuse himself always with those who were married and had complacent husbands, most of whom were years older than himself.

Only recently, now that he was thirty-three, had the Duke chosen as his companions beauties who were near his own age or younger, but they too were always already married, and it is doubtful if he ever met a marriageable girl or spoke to one.

It was the traditional pattern set by the late Monarch, Edward VII, with the "Marlborough House Set" at the end of the last century.

Once a beautiful woman had been married for some years and presented her husband with an heir, then it was more or less expected that she should enjoy a love-affair, provided that it was discreet and never in any way caused a scandal.

King Edward's liaisons, which continued up to the day of his death, were of course known to his close friends, but outside the Royal circle, the presence of the beautiful Queen Alexandra on every public occasion protected him even from the newspapers.

Perry was aware that his friend the Duke, while described as a "lady killer" by his friends, was a paragon of virtue to the outside world.

"Even if you are not inclined towards matrimony," he said now, "we shall have to look round for someone to attract your interest."

"I doubt if you will find anyone," the Duke said gloomily. "I have begun to believe they are all alike, from whatever stratum of society they may come."

He rose to his feet to walk across the room and pour himself another glass of champagne, and as he did so, he said:

"If you think Molly is extravagant, you have no idea what I am expected to provide."

"You can afford it."

"Yes, but it is decidedly irritating when you know that a woman's real interest in you is that you are a bottomless cornucopia."

The Duke spoke bitterly, and Perry laughed as he said:

"I remember an old uncle of mine saying to me once: 'At my age I expect to pay!' By altering the text a little, I can tell you that as a Duke you cannot expect anything for nothing."

The Duke did not reply and Perry went on:

"Stop thinking like an idealist and wanting to be loved for yourself. Just accept what the gods give you and be grateful for it! Incidentally, if any of The Gang heard this conversation between us, they would not believe it!"

The Duke laughed.

"If it will please you, Perry, I will admit that you are right," he said. "I am making a fool of myself. We had better go and join the others. I expect they will have arrived by now."

As he spoke, he looked at the clock over the mantelpiece and saw that it was quarter-to-eight.

"Why do we not go out after dinner?" Perry suggested. "There are masses of parties to which I expect we have all been invited. Or what about seeing the last Act at the Gaiety?"

"I have already seen that three times," the Duke said.

"There are other Theatres."

"We are dining too late for that, but if you like we could drop in at Romano's later and see if there's anybody there worth looking at."

"All right," Perry agreed, "but I should not mention it in front of Archie and the rest, or they will all want to come."

"No, we will go alone," the Duke promised.

He put down his empty glass and they walked down the lofty passage from the Library to the Blue Drawing-Room, where the Duke's friends congregated before dinner.

Tonight it was to be a stag-party, for a number of the guests had come from the races and they wanted to talk about horses, which invariably bored the opposite sex.

There were six men in the Blue Drawing-Room

and they all had glasses in their hands as the Duke and Perry came into the room.

"Hello, Alstone!" they all said, lifting their glasses. "We were beginning to think you had forgotten us."

"No, I have not done that," the Duke replied amiably. "Did you have a good day?"

A chorus of voices answered him, and he learnt that as far as the betting went, it had been a disaster, the favourites having been beaten at the post by outsiders, which nobody had thought to back.

"I am prepared to drown my sorrows," Lord Carnforth said. "But before I do so, I want your opinion, Alstone, on an argument I was having with Hugo when you came into the room."

The Duke took another glass of champagne and, seating himself in a chair, said:

"I am prepared to adjudicate. What is the subject on which you disagree?"

"We were talking about this new play by George Bernard Shaw," Sir Hugo Benson said. "It's called *Pygmalion*. Have you seen it?"

"No," the Duke replied. "What is it about?"

"It is about a phonetician who trains a flower-girl from Convent Garden so cleverly that when she can speak correctly and is well-dressed, he introduces her into Society without their being suspicious of her."

"Anything more ridiculous I have never heard!" Lord Carnforth ejaculated. "I have rather admired Shaw in the past, because at least he has some interesting ideas, but this is sheer fantasy and an insult to the public's intelligence."

"That is your opinion!" Hugo Benson replied. "I say that given a brilliant Teacher, a girl young enough to be pliable could possibly, if she had enough intelligence, deceive at any rate a large number of people."

"They would have to be half-witted, or morons!" Archie Carnforth exclaimed. "Do you imagine for one moment that any of us could be taken in by an outsider? No, of course not!"

"I suppose it might depend on how good-looking the girl was and how well-dressed," Perry hazarded.

"We are not talking about prostitutes," Archie Carnforth replied. "We are talking about making a young girl from the gutter deceive intelligent people into believing she is a Lady of Quality. That is the plot of Shaw's play, and I think it is ridiculous!"

"I rather agree with you," one of the other guests remarked. "You know as well as I do that in any society it is easy to make gaffs that are exceedingly revealing to those in the know."

"What do you mean by that?" someone enquired.

"Well, take ourselves for instance," Archie Carnforth interposed. "Supposing anybody tried to foist some outsider onto us—we would know immediately whether she was genuine or not. It would be like pretending that a paste necklace came from Cartier's. We would recognise the false. What do you think, Alstone?"

"I am inclined to agree with you," the Duke replied. "At the same time, I can understand that Shaw's play could be interesting. I must go and see it sometime."

"I should not waste your money!" Archie Carnforth said. "The whole thing is rubbish from start to finish!"

"I disagree with you," Hugo Benson said sharply,

"for apart from anything else, I think women are so adaptable that like a chameleon they can take their colour from whomever they are with."

"That again is sheer nonsense!" Lord Carnforth said aggressively. "Women have to stick, as they always have, to their own environment, to the people with whom they have ties of blood and brain. Outside that, they are helpless and they stand out as obviously as a pimple on the nose."

Hugo rose to his feet.

"That is the most damned silly statement I have ever heard!" he said. "All through history women have acclimatised themselves and adjusted themselves into societies to which they have been introduced by circumstances. What is more, they have been successful in queening it, literally in some cases, over those with whom they have associated."

"I rather agree with Hugo on that," the Duke remarked.

"I doubt if he can substantiate such a statement," Archie Carnforth said.

"But can you?" another man asked.

"Well, look at it this way," Lord Carnforth replied, "we know one another very well and so do the women whom Alstone entertains as he so generously entertains us. Do you imagine that a stranger with an entirely different background, suddenly thrown in amongst us, would not stand out, isolated in a most embarrassing manner, and be a crashing bore as far as we were concerned?"

"I see what you mean," someone remarked, "they would be out-of-it. They would not understand our jokes or be able to follow the conversation, and it might in fact be as embarrassing for us as for them."

"Exactly!" Archie continued. "And Hugo can have no answer to that."

"Of course I have an answer," Sir Hugo snapped. "No social set is static. New people enter it, both men and women, and though at first they may feel slightly strange, they are very quickly absorbed."

"I still say it is not easy, unless they were born into the same social world and have the same interests as those with whom they are associating," Archie Carnforth retorted.

He looked round the room before he added:

"Can you imagine if we had a man here tonight who had never been racing, never played Bridge, not been to a Public School, and had never met any of us before? Well, all I can say is that I would feel sorry for the poor devil."

"But suppose he was a woman?" someone asked, laughing.

"Even if she was pretty," Lord Carnforth replied, "or beautiful, if you like, she would still find herself at a loss if she did not know anybody we know and had never been to any of the places we go to, and did not appreciate that Alstone is the best-looking Duke in the whole of *Debrett!*"

"She would be blind if she did not realise that!" Perry said, and there was a roar of laughter.

"Where women are concerned it is obviously easier than in the case of a man," Hugo Benson said, when the laughter subsided, "and that's why I say that Shaw's contention in *Pygmalion* is perfectly possible. The Professor took much time and trouble to teach Eliza Doolittle to speak correctly, but after all, he was a phonetician. Supposing *we* started with someone who was not born a Lady. Do you not suppose that very quickly she would feel at home with all of us? And we would accept her without any more question?"

"Impossible! Completely and absolutely impossible!" Archie Carnforth said. "You are talking through your hat, Hugo! Can you see the type of woman you suggest, being able to talk to Daisy or Kitty without them seeing through her and having her in tears within ten minutes of her appearance?"

"If she was pretentious, of course!" Hugo Benson said. "But if she was very young, like Shaw's Eliza Doolittle, then I think they would accept her."

"Very young?" Archie Carnforth queried. "Good God, have you ever seen a débutante when she first leaves the School-Room, gauche, inarticulate, hopelessly shy? It always astounds me how the mere act of marriage turns them into the witty, charming creatures we all find so alluring."

"I suppose marriage has somewhat the same effect as Shaw's phonetician," Hugo conceded. "At the same time, we are straying from the point. I am saying that it would be possible to train a complete outsider, like that damned horse that won this afternoon, to beat the favourite, if it was put into the right race."

The Duke was listening and it was obvious that he was rather interested in what Sir Hugo was suggesting.

"What you are saying," he said after a moment, "is that if a young girl was introduced into our particular circle, she would not remain gauche and tongue-tied as Archie suggests, but would soon be as polished and assured as we think ourselves to be."

"As we *are!*" Perry averred.

"Very well. As we are!" the Duke conceded.

"That is right," Hugo said. "You have put it very well, Alstone; and what has Archie to say to that?"

"I say you are off your head and such a thing is completely impossible except on the Stage. If you are so sure of yourself, Hugo, you had better prove it, as no-one will believe you otherwise."

There was a surprised silence. Then the Duke said in an amused voice:

"That is a challenge, Hugo, and I for one am prepared to put a bet on it!"

"So am I!" a man exclaimed. "Who will make a book on it?"

"I will," Perry announced.

He had seen that the idea interested the Duke, and he thought it could be an excellent way to rouse him from his introspective mood.

'At least this is something new,' he thought to himself, 'but Heaven knows if we can make it last.'

He walked across the room to an elegant Louis XIV writing-table, took a piece of heavily embossed crested writing-paper from the velvet box in which it was kept, and picked up a quill-pen.

"Now then, Hugo," he said, "you are not going to rat on us, I hope?"

"I have no intention of doing that," Sir Hugo replied sharply, "but give me a moment to think."

"What we are asking you to do," the Duke said, as if he felt it should all be put clearly, "is to produce a girl—to save time she can be a Lady by birth—who has had no contact with the Social World, no experience of anything which is familiar to us. Then, in a very short space of time, she has to become so much at home in our company that we accept her as one of ourselves. Is that right?"

Hugo Benson nodded.

Lord Carnforth said with a smile:

"I am prepared to bet a thousand-to-one that Hugo fails dismally in his extremely speculative aspirations."

"I am prepared to back you in that," the man sitting next to him said. "All right, Hugo, I will bet a 'monkey' that the whole experiment fails utterly."

"I accept your bets," Sir Hugo said. "What about you, Alstone?"

"I intend to be the Judge," the Duke replied, "and I think we must make it clear from the very beginning, Perry, that the Judge's decision is final."

"Yes, of course," Perry agreed. "Any more bets? I personally intend to support Hugo."

"Thank you, Perry; I have a feeling I shall need a friend."

"You can count on me too," another man remarked, but three other guests bet small sums against Sir Hugo.

"This is going to cost you rather a lot of money," Perry said as he totted it up.

"I am not going to lose," Sir Hugo said, "because although I swear to you I had not thought of it when this argument started, I think I know exactly the right girl to take part in this experiment."

"We will want to know all about her," the Duke said, "to make quite certain that you are not getting off to an unfair start."

"I am not doing that," Sir Hugo replied, "because I have not seen the girl in question for three years."

"Who is she?"

"She happens to be my niece."

There was silence for a moment. Then Lord Carnforth said:

"We had better know every detail before we accept Hugo's entry for the contest."

"I am perfectly prepared to give them to you," Hugo Benson answered. "The girl in question is the daughter of my brother, who you may or may not remember was a Parson, the Vicar of a small Parish in Worcestershire."

Someone laughed, then said:

"Sorry, Hugo, but I had no idea that your brother was a Parson. It is quite the most ludicrous thing I have ever heard that you, the most dashing man-about-town, should have a brother in the Church!"

"It is true," Sir Hugo replied, "and when he died, I sent his daughter to a School in Rome."

"Why did you do that?"

"She seemed a rather artistic, quiet, studious girl, and I thought she would have a better education there. Also, to be honest, it saved me any worry over holidays."

"You mean," the Duke said perceptively, "that Kitty did not know what to do with your niece."

"Exactly!" Sir Hugo replied. "Kitty dislikes young girls and has no use for them."

Everyone listening understood only too well that Kitty Benson, who was always engaged in some intense love-affair, would certainly not want a young girl in her house, especially one who was unsophisticated and might even be censorious of her aunt's behaviour.

What was more, they all realised that Kitty was reaching the age at which she had no wish to be the aunt of anybody.

"So you sent her away to Rome," the Duke said. "What happened then?"

"She has grown up," Sir Hugo replied, "and the school, which incidentally is a kind of Convent, will not keep her any longer."

"A Convent!" Perry exclaimed.

"It is a Convent-School," Sir Hugo explained, "where the Nuns teach some of the subjects, but there are outside Teachers for a number of others. The pupils are predominantly Catholic, but they take girls from other religions and I had no difficulty in arranging for Lorena to go there."

"So Lorena is her name?" the Duke remarked.

Sir Hugo nodded, then turned to the others and said:

"I have been quite frank with you, gentlemen. I have not seen her for three years, and she was then, I thought, attractive in a rather unusual way. But anything may have happened in the meantime."

"What you are hoping," someone said, "is that your dark horse will turn out to be a beauty."

"Of course I am hoping that," Sir Hugo agreed. "But I am a sportsman and I hope you realise that I am giving everybody a sporting chance to prove that I am wrong, and it will certainly cost me a packet if I am!"

"At least you are right about that!" Perry said, looking at the list in his hand.

"Will you tell us a little more about your niece?" the Duke asked.

"To tell you the truth, I know very little more," Sir Hugo replied. "She has written to me dutifully, and they have been quite interesting letters. She is obviously intelligent, and I hope well educated."

"Not too well educated—I hope!" a man ejaculated. "If there is one thing I really dislike, it is a clever woman!"

"She will have to be clever," Perry objected, "if she is to fulfil all Hugo's hopes of her."

"Yes, of course, I had forgotten that."

"But she may be as stupid, tongue-tied, and shy as Archie anticipates," Sir Hugo said. "All I am hoping is that she has a little of the 'chip of the old block' in her and will romp home to a triumphant finish."

"I think you are asking too much," the Duke said with a smile. "But if she is like you, Hugo, she will bowl over Society as apparently Shaw's heroine did."

There was certainly some truth in this, for Sir Hugo Benson's name was a byword of smartness and *savoir-faire*.

He was in some ways the modern equivalent of the Georgian Dandies and Bucks who had centred round the Prince Regent.

King Edward had found him one of the most amusing of his friends, and a party seldom took place at Marlborough House, and subsequently at Buckingham Palace, without Sir Hugo being there.

When the King died, Sir Hig had attached himself to the Duke and enlivened what was known as the Windlemere Set, bringing his wit, his sense of humour, and his originality to those who tried to keep the Duke as their special property.

He was now over forty but he looked much younger, and his good figure and the smartness of his dress was the envy of every ambitious young man in the Social World.

It was so like Hugo to suggest some new amusement, Perry thought as they walked into dinner, and he told himself that for the moment this was the answer to the Duke's cry for something new.

There was no doubt that the Duke was interested, because as he sat down at the head of the table, with Sir Hugo on his right, he asked:

"When does our experiment start?"

"That is what I want to know," Lord Carnforth said. "And there is to be no cheating, Hugo, in that you coach the girl beforehand!"

"Do you mean that?" Sir Hugo enquired. "If I cannot talk to her and tell her what is expected, it will be a very severe handicap as far as I am concerned."

"I think she needs a handicap because she is your niece," someone said, laughing.

"As Adjudicator, I cannot allow Hugo to have to carry too much weight," said the Duke.

"I can see that Archie is really suspicious of me," Sir Hugo said, "so I am prepared to take a chance which you certainly should appreciate."

"What is that?" Lord Carnforth asked.

"I will allow anyone you choose to come with me to meet Lorena when she arrives the day after tomorrow at Victoria Station. Then it will be up to you to decide where we take her and how you all meet her for the first time."

There was silence for a moment, then the Duke said:

"I was going to suggest that she come here, but the day after tomorrow is Friday and I had intended to go down to Mere."

"Of course!" Archie Carnforth exclaimed. "Mere would be the perfect place to try out her paces."

"I think," Sir Hugo said with a smile, "she will

find Mere so overwhelming, so grandiose, that she will be stricken dumb the moment she sees it."

"Can you think of somewhere better to go?" Archie asked.

"No; and once again, I accept the challenge," Sir Hugo said. "Alstone is right. A party at Mere would be a severe test for any woman, let alone an inexperienced girl, and will prove my point once and for all."

"Personally, I think you are crazy, even though I am supporting you," Perry said. "But if you pick up your niece at Victoria Station, you can then drive in one of Alstone's cars to Mere in an hour and a half."

"I agree," Sir Hugo said, "and you can send anybody you like, Archie, to accompany us, so that you shall know that I am not 'doping the horse before the race begins.' "

"I will consider who it should be," Archie Carnforth replied.

"Take your time," Sir Hugo said good-humouredly. "We should arrive at Mere at about six o'clock and give the child time to change for dinner."

He looked round the table with a smile which seemed to be one of self-satisfaction.

'He is betting on a certainty,' Perry thought to himself, 'or else he is more of a reckless gambler than even I imagined.'

However he was not particularly concerned about Sir Hugo, for he was thinking that for the moment, at any rate, the boredom had vanished from the Duke's eyes.

*   *   *

As the train reached the outskirts of London, Lorena began to collect her things and the two other girls in the carriage with her did the same.

The Governess who had accompanied them all the way from Rome said sharply in broken English:

"Now, *Mesdemoiselles,* do not leave anything behind. You do not wish to lose your possessions."

"No, indeed, *Mademoiselle,*" one of the girls replied, "although of course my mother has some wonderful gowns waiting for me, and especially the one I am to wear at my presentation."

"I wonder whether we shall be presented in the same Drawing-Room," the other girl said. "What about you, Lorena?"

"I do not know what will happen to me," Lorena answered in a soft voice. "You see, I have no mother to present me. In fact, both my parents are dead."

"I had forgotten you were an orphan!" one of the girls exclaimed. "Oh, poor Lorena! But perhaps I shall be able to see you if you are in London."

"Again, I have no idea where I shall be," Lorena replied. "My uncle only writes to me occasionally and tells me very little news. It is rather frightening, stepping into a new life and having no idea what it will be like or even where I shall be living."

"It sounds horrid to me," one of her friends remarked, "but I expect you will be all right. You are too clever to be anything else."

"I wish that were true," Lorena smiled, "but I know that my aunt, at any rate, is not going to be very impressed by book-learning."

As she spoke, she thought of her Aunt Kitty as she had last seen her, exquisitely dressed but with what Lorena thought was a hard expression on her pretty face.

Lorena had asked her quite innocently if she would be allowed to come home from Rome in the holidays.

"Come home?" Lady Benson had said in a sharp voice. "If by home you mean here, the answer is no! You will stay in Rome until you are fully educated, and that will take at least the next three years."

"All that time?" Lorena had asked in dismay.

"You are a very lucky girl!" Lady Benson had said. "It costs your uncle a great deal of money to send you to Rome. You will have an excellent education—far better, I am sure, than your father would ever have been able to afford. You might at least be grateful."

"I am very, very grateful," Lorena had replied. "It is just the idea of being with . . . strangers and of . . . knowing nobody."

"As you are an orphan, you have to get used to strangers, as you call them," Lady Benson had said. "And let me make it quite clear, Lorena, that I have no time and certainly no inclination to chaperone a young girl. I do not like children and have none of my own, thank goodness!"

"I . . . understand," Lorena had said humbly.

When she had left her uncle's house the next morning to travel with some other girls who were going to Rome, she had not been able to say good-bye to her aunt because she had not yet been called.

Uncle Hugo had always been very kind to her but she found him rather frightening.

He was so unlike her father in every way and it was strange to think that they were brothers.

She had learnt when she was quite young that her father had chosen to go into the Church in the teeth of opposition from his father and from his elder brother.

He had heard a call to help other people to worship God as he did, and no argument would make him join the family Regiment, as had been intended.

When still a Curate he had married the daughter of a country Squire who was as unworldy as himself, but they loved each other in a way which made anywhere they lived seem to have an aura of happiness which no money could buy.

After they were both dead, Lorena knew that her special world, which had always seemed to be filled with sunshine, music, and laughter, had gone forever.

It had taken her some time to adjust herself to School-life, and not even the Nuns had realised how much she suffered or how home-sick she was for a home that was no longer there, and how she longed for her mother and father, who were together in a place which she could not reach.

They thought her very quiet.

Then the sweetness of her nature, her understanding of other people's problems, and her unusual perceptiveness, which made her different from other girls, gradually made those who at first had barely noticed her aware that she was not only there but important to them personally.

Anyone in trouble turned to Lorena instinctively.

She listened to the worries not only of the girls of her own age but of everyone else in the Convent—the visiting Teachers, the Italian servants who

were always ready to talk, and even the Nuns themselves.

She had a capacity for listening, and although
she might say little, she made those to whom she
listened feel that they had found a solution to their
problems.

It was largely because she made them find
within themselves the answers they needed, a
quality and a virtue which finally commended itself
to the Mother Superior.

"It has been a happiness for all of us to have you
here," she told Lorena when she said good-bye.
"You have developed a great deal, for which I hope
we can take some credit, but I think actually what
you have, my child, is something God gives us at
birth, and we either develop it or are not aware of
its existence."

Lorena smiled.

"I hope I have . . . developed, Reverend Mother."

"You have, and it is something that will stand
you in good stead now that you are going out into
the world. I understand you are not yet certain
where you will live or who will look after you."

"I am . . . sure my uncle will find . . . someone," Lorena said hesitatingly.

The Reverend Mother knew she was apprehensive.

"You must trust in God," she said, "and remember, child, always to use your instinct. It will
tell you what is right and what is wrong, and it is
the way that God speaks to us, especially if we
need His guidance."

"I shall remember, Reverend Mother," Lorena
said.

During the long journey across France, she

thought over what had been said. She knew that her instincts would have to help her in a great number of ways which perhaps the Reverend Mother did not envisage.

There was nothing in the books she had read at the Convent to tell her anything of the Social World to which she knew her uncle belonged and in which she had no doubt that her aunt would not wish her to play any part.

Her father had often laughed about his brother's important place in Society and the way he associated with Royalty as if it was his right.

"How I should have hated it!" Lorena had heard him say often enough.

"It must be very interesting, Papa," she had hazarded.

"It depends on what you want out of life," her father replied. "The superficial trappings of pomp and circumstance certainly are not for me. But if they make my brother Hugo happy, I am the last person to tell him he should seek anything different."

"It must be fascinating to know the King and the beautiful Queen Alexandra," Lorena said.

"There is a great deal of glamour about them," her father conceded. "At the same time, they are people, just like old Mr. and Mrs. Briggs, who I am calling on now because they will be celebrating their Golden Wedding Anniversary next week."

He smiled before he added:

"Not that there will be much gold about it, but I am sure your mother is prepared to bake them a cake."

"Of course, dearest," her mother replied. "I have already planned it, and as I do not think the icing would look very pretty in yellow, I have bought some golden candles to put on top of it."

"You think of everything, darling," her husband said.

He kissed her before he left the Vicarage.

'They were so happy,' Lorena thought.

She wondered if Uncle Hugo could possibly be happy in the same way with Aunt Kitty, who had said she "had no children, thank goodness."

Her father and mother had always deeply regretted that they had only one child.

"I would like to have had a dozen children as they would have made your father so happy," her mother had said once. "But God had other ideas, and after you were born, the Doctors told me I could have no more."

"How can I make up to you for all the children you have not had?" Lorena asked.

Her mother put her arms round her and held her close.

"You have done that already," she said. "Daddy and I are perfectly content to have one adorable daughter and a very pretty one at that!"

"I shall never be as pretty as you, Mummy."

"It is fun to be pretty," her mother answered, "but it is wonderful when the man you love thinks you are beautiful."

"That is what Daddy thinks."

"Yes, I know," her mother answered, "and that is why I am not only the luckiest woman in the world but also the happiest."

'That is what I want in my life,' Lorena thought as the train carried her towards London, 'to be as happy as Mummy and Daddy were.'

She was still thinking of them when the train

drew slowly along the platform at Victoria Station and she saw her Uncle Hugo, looking extremely elegant, his top-hat on his head and a carnation in his button-hole, waiting on the platform with another gentleman beside him.

Chapter Two

Waiting on the platform, Sir Hugo admitted to himself that he was apprehensive.

He had not really meant to get so involved in a wager which might easily cost him a great deal of money.

He had had a lot to drink at the races, and although he was never drunk—he was far too fastidious for that—he thought afterwards that it must have slightly distorted his common sense.

The only reason he had entered into the argument was that Archie Carnforth had annoyed him.

He was in fact the only close friend of the Duke's for whom Sir Hugo had little liking.

He was so self-opinionated, so absolutely certain that he was always right and that his opponents on whatever subject must therefore necessarily be wrong.

He had been particularly irritating at the races, where, when each one of the outsiders won, he lectured the rest of the party on how they should have been knowledgeable enough to have anticipated that that particular horse had a chance.

Although he was a well-known race-horse owner he seldom placed a bet, and Hugo Benson and a number of other people found that in itself distinctly tiresome.

Anyway, Sir Hugo thought, he had let himself in for what promised to be a difficult and uncomfortable visit to Mere, and instead of looking forward, as he usually did, to being with the Duke and his friends, he was in fact definitely apprehensive.

Too late, he thought that he should have insisted on keeping Lorena for a week in London, so that he could at least dress her suitably before he presented her to his opponents in the contest.

That was what Professor Higgins in *Pygmalion* had done, and Sir Hugo thought that he had been singularly remiss in forgetting that the clothes in which a woman was dressed were perhaps more important than anything else.

'I have made a fool of myself,' he thought ruefully.

And as if he sensed what he was feeling, Perry, who was with him, said:

"Cheer up, Hugo! Your traditional good luck will stand you in good stead."

Sir Hugo laughed.

"Is it so obvious that I am anticipating the worst?"

"You have spoken barely a word since we left White's," Perry replied, "and that is unusual, to say the least of it!"

Over dinner at Mere, they had had quite a fight

as to who should actually accompany Sir Hugo to the station.

Lord Carnforth had suggested that he himself should go, but that had been turned down because, as Hugo Benson said, he was so deeply involved that he might easily contrive in one way or another to make Lorena afraid and shy of what was waiting for her.

Finally the Duke decided who it was to be, saying that as Judge he was appointing Perry, believing that he could rely on him to be impartial as it was a question of sportsmanship.

"He may be supporting you, Hugo," the Duke said, "but at the same time he will feel responsible to me in seeing that you take no unfair advantage on the way to Mere."

"If you ask me, I am carrying far too much weight in this race," Sir Hugo complained. "Firstly, I am not allowed to warn the child; secondly, she will have a stranger, in the shape of Perry, listening to every word she says; and thirdly, she will already be tired after journeying all the way from Rome."

"I will take all those things into consideration," Lord Carnforth said in a manner which set Sir Hugo's teeth on edge.

Now Sir Hugo said to Perry:

"I have just realised that I should at least have been allowed to dress Lorena for the part she is to play."

"That is the wrong expression," Perry said quickly. "She is not allowed to know it is a part. If she puts on an act, you know as well as I do that it will be obvious to everybody."

Sir Hugo nodded.

"At the same time," he said, "she will, I suppose, be wearing only the clothes she has worn at School."

He groaned as he thought how badly dressed were the School-girls he had sometimes seen parading crocodile-fashion through Hyde Park.

If Lorena looked anything like them, he decided, he would call the whole thing off and refuse to take her to Mere.

"I am not going to make a laughing-stock of myself," he said aloud.

There was a look of surprise on Perry's face, and he explained:

"I am aware that I made a vital error from the word 'go.' Let us make it quite clear, Perry, that if the child is plain, spotty, and badly dressed, you go to Mere without me. I am not going to have Archie crowing over me from the moment he sees her and every time she opens her mouth."

"I see no reason why she should not be attractive, if she is your niece," Perry said disarmingly.

"Archie is right," Sir Hugo said gloomily, "unfledged girls of that age are gauche, stupid, and shy. Why the devil did I get into this mess in the first place?"

"Because it annoyed you that Archie was so dogmatic."

Sir Hugo laughed.

"That is true," he admitted.

"Well, I am interested in this competition, or whatever you like to call it," Perry said, "not only because I agree with you, and Archie can be infuriatingly dictatorial, but also because it appears to amuse Alstone."

Sir Hugo smiled.

"I imagined that was why you were supporting me."

"He is bored, Hugo," Perry said. "It seems incredible, but he is!"

"That is Daisy's fault," Sir Hugo replied. "She has been presuming on his affections for far too long. I could have warned her that he was chafing at the bit."

"Why did you not do so?"

Sir Hugo grinned.

"Daisy has done her best on several occasions to 'put a spoke in my wheel.'"

"So it was 'tit-for-tat'!"

"Exactly! I am hoping that once Alstone is free of her, he will find a woman who is more amenable, and certainly one who is more pleasant to his friends."

"Have you anyone in mind?" Perry enquired.

"As a matter of fact there is someone," Sir Hugo answered, "who I nearly suggested might be invited to Mere this week, until I thought it might confuse the issue."

"Yes, of course," Perry agreed. "We want Alstone to concentrate on the contest. She had better come another time, and certainly not when Daisy is there."

"That is what I thought," Sir Hugo agreed. "As Daisy is to be at Mere this week, there is no room for anyone else."

The two men smiled knowingly at each other.

The Countess of Hellingford had been overbearing and, they thought, at times disloyal to both of them.

Because they were genuinely fond of the Duke,

they felt it important to protect him from anyone who exploited him too obviously, and that was particularly true of women.

Because he was so rich, those he favoured invariably took advantage of his generosity, which was indeed understandable up to a certain point.

But Daisy Hellingford was greedy, and it was not only the diamonds she wore round her neck that the Duke had paid for, but the horses she rode and the cars in which she was driven.

She also expected him to provide a great many other things that were not usually in the category of permissible gifts from a man to his mistress.

Daisy was by no means impoverished: her husband, who was conveniently big-game hunting in Africa, was well off and owned a large Estate in Gloucestershire.

That he was not travelling without female companionship enabled Daisy to gain the sympathy of the women in playing the part of a wronged wife.

But Sir Hugo and Perry were convinced that if there was anything irregular about the whole arrangement, it was of Daisy's doing.

"I can tell you one thing," Perry said now, "when they do part, we will make damned sure that someone at Mere counts the Van Dykes and the collection of snuff-boxes."

Sir Hugo laughed.

They were both thinking of another of the Duke's lady-loves, from whom he had parted with much recrimination on her side, only to find after the break was final that quite a number of the miniatures which were family heirlooms had mysteriously disappeared.

They had been returned after quite a large

amount of money had changed hands in compensation.

"Here comes the train!" Sir Hugo exclaimed.

Perry thought with slight amusement that his friend was definitely tense and it was so unlike Sir Hugo to be worried about anything.

He was one of those people who always seem to be riding high, immune from the small and tiresome anxieties of the common herd, so this was certainly an unusual condition for him to be in.

The train puffed slowly to the end of the platform and Perry found that he too was intensely curious as to what Lorena would look like.

It would certainly be great fun and a triumph if she was as attractive as he and her uncle hoped, but his common sense told him that it was very unlikely.

She might not be quite as bad as Archie Carnforth depicted, but he was right in saying that a School-girl, any School-girl, would be out-of-place at Mere with the men and women who were among the most sophisticated to be found in Europe.

Now that King Edward was dead and the hostesses who had presided over the brilliant and glittering Salons that had been so much a part of his Reign had gone, there was only the Windlemere Set left to glitter with what was not only a social but an intellectual brilliance.

The women were chosen for their beauty, the men for their brains.

Like Sir Hugo, Perry was wondering how they could ever have got involved in such an absurd idea as to imagine that they could perform their own version of *Pygmalion* among themselves.

'It is all that damned man Shaw's fault,' he

thought. 'I believe he has been a trouble-maker all his life, one way or another.'

As the passengers were pouring out of the train, Sir Hugo stood watching them, leaning lightly on his malacca cane, with his polished top-hat at an angle on his head and looking completely at his ease.

Only Perry knew that what he was feeling was very differently.

Then Sir Hugo said almost beneath his breath: "Here she is!"

Perry turned his head to see a girl approaching them.

For a moment he thought she was far too young to be Lorena, who he knew was eighteen; then as she drew nearer, he was sure of it.

But she had seen Sir Hugo and was running towards him with a little cry.

"Uncle Hugo!" she exclaimed, a lilt in her voice. "I was hoping you would come to meet me. It is lovely to see you and lovely to be home again."

Sir Hugo kissed her cheek, then said:

"I am glad to have you back, Lorena. Let me look at you—you do not appear to have grown very much."

He held her from him at arm's-length, and Perry knew he had another reason for inspecting her, besides the fact that she was his niece.

Then as he looked at her closely Perry drew in his breath.

If he had hoped for something different from the ordinary School-girl, his hopes had certainly been fulfilled.

Lorena was not in the slightest like any School-girl he had ever seen before.

Looking at her face, it was difficult to believe she could be more than fifteen or sixteen, but her body beneath the blue travelling-gown she wore was sweetly curved.

But for the moment Perry was concerned only with her face, and it was not difficult to realise that she was in fact not pretty but lovely, yet in a different way from other women.

It was the fashion, as it had been from the beginning of the century, for the beauties who were most admired to be tall, fair, blue-eyed, and somewhat Junoesque as regards their figures.

Lorena was none of these things.

She was small, slim, and had the pale fairness of a dawn sky, while her eyes were the transparent blue of a thrush's egg.

Because she looked so young, her face should have been round, but instead her chin was pointed, her small nose was very straight, and her lips curved.

'She reminds me of something,' Perry thought, 'but I cannot put a name to it.'

Then as Sir Hugo introduced him and she smiled, he felt as if she held the sunshine in her strange eyes and her smile held a spontaneous delight that somehow reminded him of his childhood.

"This is Peregrine Gillingham," Sir Hugo was saying, "an old friend of mine who is accompanying us on the journey we are now taking to the country."

"To the country, Uncle Hugo!" Lorena exclaimed. "How lovely! Where are we going?"

"To stay with another friend of mine, the Duke of Windlemere," Sir Hugo answered, "at his

house, which is one of the finest in England. I
think you will enjoy seeing it."

"It sounds very exciting!" Lorena said. "But
more exciting than anything else is to be with you."

The porters found Lorena's luggage, which
Perry noticed consisted only of two small leather
trunks, and they went slowly along the platform,
Lorena apologising that the train was late owing to
the fact that they had had a rough crossing of the
Channel.

"Were you sea-sick?" Sir Hugo enquired.

"No, but a great many other people were,"
Lorena replied. "I was so sorry for them, but
there was nothing I could do, so I stayed up on
deck."

"That sounds very sensible," Sir Hugo approved.

They had moved out of the station and found
waiting outside two large, very impressive cars.
The first was driven by a chauffeur in dark green
uniform, and beside him was a footman wearing
the Windlemere livery.

The other car, behind it, was for the luggage and
it also carried Sir Hugo's and Perry's valets.

Lorena stepped into the first car, and as she
seated herself on the back seat she said:

"This too is very exciting! I have only been in a
car three or four times since I left England."

"Are you telling me there are no cars in Rome?"
Perry asked.

"Oh, no, there are plenty of them," Lorena replied, "but the Nuns expected us to walk everywhere, and I only went in a car when one of the
other pupils invited me out. But most people in
Rome prefer to drive in open carriages. It is so

much easier to see the beauty of the city when
you are not going too fast."

"I am sure that is true," Perry said, "and when
we go tearing about the countryside at a hundred
miles an hour, we shall see nothing but our own
dust, and hear nothing but the roar of engines."

"I prefer horses," Sir Hugo said, "but it is certainly far quicker to travel as we are now; and
although the train was late we shall still have time
to change for dinner without rushing."

As if changing for dinner made him think of
Lorena's clothes again, be turned to his niece to
say:

"I hope you have something attractive to wear.
This will be a very smart party."

She did not answer for a moment, and Perry
had the idea that Sir Hugo was holding his breath.

"I think," Lorena replied, "that the clothes I
bought in Rome with the money you so kindly
sent me every year are attractive, but perhaps
they will not be smart enough for your friends."

As she spoke, she remembered how her father
had always described his brother's friends as being
rich and smart and how he had laughed about
their "superficial trappings of pomp and circumstance."

There was suddenly a worried look in her blue
eyes, and as if Sir Hugo could not bear to make
her anxious of what lay ahead or to feel self-
conscious, he said quickly:

"I am certain you have good taste, and I like
what you are wearing now."

It was, Perry thought, a very simple get-up, but
in some way which he could not explain, it was
completely right on Lorena, just as her travelling-

hat suited her as it turned back from her face and
gave her the little-girl look which he had noticed
the moment he saw her.

The fashion was for large hats copiously decorated with feathers and flowers. But Lorena's hat
was trimmed only with blue ribbons and looked
rather like a halo as it circled her small head.

The cars were soon clear of London and Lorena
leant forward to watch the countryside as they
passed through it.

"I had forgotten England was so green," she
said, almost as if she was speaking to herself,
"and the trees are beautiful. I know now how
much I have missed it all these last three years."

"Have you been home-sick?" Sir Hugo enquired.

"I think that is the right word," Lorena answered, "even though I no longer have a home;
but perhaps one naturally longs for one's own
environment, for the land to which one belongs
by birth."

Perry was startled.

She was saying in different words what Archie
Carnforth had averred about environment. Hers
had been a Vicarage in the country, and that was
as far removed from Mere as the North Pole from
the South.

As the cars seemed to eat up the miles swiftly
and smoothly, Perry noticed that Lorena did not
chatter as most other women would have done.
He was sure Sir Hugo appreciated the fact that
she was quiet.

It was always a bore to talk above the noise of
a car, but he wondered if, in fact, Lorena was
silent because she had nothing to say, or if she

was sensitive enough to realise that men did not wish to talk in such circumstances.

They had almost reached Mere before Sir Hugo said:

"I think I ought to tell you to expect quite a large party, who are all close friends of the Duke, and I know that you will be sorry that your aunt cannot be here this week, as she had to visit her mother, who is ill."

"Oh, poor Aunt Kitty! I am sorry!" Lorena said.

Even as she spoke she felt that it was wrong of her to feel relieved.

She had not forgotten the way her aunt had spoken to her before she had been sent off to Rome.

She had said then that she had no wish to chaperone a young girl and doubtless she had not changed her mind.

It had made Lorena worry what was to happen to her and where she would be sent when she reached England, but it was a joy to know that she would have a week alone with her uncle wherever they might be staying.

Although they had been so different in temperament, he was her beloved father's brother and there was now, although Sir Hugo would not have agreed, a resemblance which Lorena could see even if no-one else would have been able to do so.

It was, she thought, in the way he smiled, the way he spoke, and sometimes in the expression in his eyes.

But her father had not been smart in that he did not dress with the meticulous elegance which she had always known was characteristic of her uncle.

Nevertheless, because they were brothers there was a family resemblance that made her feel that she had come home and that some part of her family, if only a small part, was waiting for her.

"I shall like meeting your friends, Uncle Hugo," she said, "and will you please tell me if I do anything wrong? I would not want you to be ashamed of me."

"I am quite certain I shall not be that," Sir Hugo replied. "What I am going to suggest is that as soon as we arrive, you go up to your room and take your time in changing into your best gown. First appearances are always important."

Lorena laughed.

"Now you are making me nervous, although I am quite certain no-one will even notice me. But I want to look at all the interesting and exciting people that you know. Mummy sometimes used to read their names out of the Court Circular and it always sounded to me like listening to a fairy-story."

The way she spoke was so ingenuous and natural that Perry said:

"You are quite right, Lorena, that is just what it is, and when you see the Duke you will know that he is Prince Charming, though your uncle is a good runner-up for that role!"

"You flatter me," Sir Hugo said, laughing.

Lorena clapped her hands together.

"What you are saying is that like Cinderella I am going to a Ball, and what could be a better coach than the one in which we are travelling? Although of course it ought to have six white ponies to pull it."

"In which case," Perry replied, "we should not

only miss the Prince's Banquet, but it would be after midnight before we arrived!"

Lorena laughed with delight.

"That would be too disappointing and I would not even have a glass slipper to leave behind. Not that I have a pair to wear this evening!"

"Never mind," Sir Hugo said. "Make yourself look as pretty as possible and I will come and collect you when it is time to go down to dinner."

"Thank you, Uncle Hugo. It is so kind of you, and I promise I will not keep you waiting."

"You had better not do that," Perry said. "The Duke is very punctilious about time, and if there is one thing that makes him angry it is people being late for dinner."

The way he spoke made Lorena look at him reflectively, and he asked:

"What are you thinking?"

"You sound almost as if you are afraid of the Duke," she answered frankly. "Perhaps after all he is not Prince Charming but the Demon King!"

Both Perry and Sir Hugo laughed.

"Wait until you see him!" Perry said after a moment. "You will not say that then."

Lorena thought Mere indeed looked like a Fairy-Palace from the first moment she saw it. The huge roof surmounted by the Duke's standard was silhouetted against the sky and she stared wide-eyed at the largest and most famous Robert Adam mansion in the whole of Great Britain.

Its huge dome, the wings springing out from the centre building, its Corinthian-column entrance, and the hundreds of windows gleaming golden in the setting sun were not only so beautiful but also so impressive that Lorena told herself that this was the England she had always wanted to see.

Her father might have disparaged the life that his brother lived, but she had felt it had a glamour and a mystique about it that stimulated her imagination and even coloured her dreams.

Now for the first time she would see for herself the England that had made the Eighteenth Century a time of notable architectural development, the England which in the Reign of George IV had set a standard of luxury and elegance which was the envy of all Europe.

Because that was a period of history that Lorena most enjoyed, she had hoped almost against hope that the England which had become even more prosperous in Queen Victoria's time had not changed too drastically after her death.

There had been few books in the School-Library to describe to her the history of England since the beginning of the century and she had been afraid that by the time she returned home she would find the grandeur and splendour had passed with the death of Edward VII.

Even at the Convent she had heard talk of its being "the end of an era" and that King George and Queen Mary were very different from the flamboyant Monarch who had been called the "Uncle of Europe."

But here, right in front of her eyes, was the splendour and glory she wanted to see.

When they entered the huge marble Hall with statues of gods and goddesses set in niches in the walls, Lorena stared round her with delight.

The footmen with their powdered wigs and knee-breeches were exactly what she had expected,

and when on her uncle's instructions she was escorted up the huge carved staircase to where a
Housekeeper in rustling black silk with a silver
chatelaine falling from her waist was waiting for
her, Lorena wanted to exclaim with joy that it was
all she had hoped for.

"Will you come this way, Miss?" the Housekeeper was saying. "I'll take you to your bedroom,
which, as I thought you'd wish, is close to that of
your uncle."

"It is so kind of you to think of it," Lorena replied.

Then as if she could not help herself she exclaimed:

"What a wonderful house this is!"

"I'm glad you should think so, Miss."

"And how long have you been here?" Lorena
enquired. "I'm afraid I did not hear your name.
Perhaps you would tell it to me."

"Mrs. Kingston, Miss. I'm called 'Mrs.' although
I've never been married."

"I expect you look on this house as your home,"
Lorena said, and the Housekeeper smiled at her.

"That's true, Miss. We all of us who have been
here many years feel as if Mere belongs to us as
well as to His Grace. But then, as almost everyone
employed here was born on the Estate, it's very
much a family business, so to speak."

She laughed a little at her own joke, and Lorena
said:

"How comforting that sounds! And you would
miss it very much if it were not here, just as I miss
my home and my family."

"I understand your parents are dead, Miss,"
Mrs. Kingston said. "It's very sad for you, but I

feel sure Sir Hugo will look after you. We're all very fond of him here at Mere."

As she spoke, she showed Lorena into a bed-room which made her again exclaim with delight.

There was a four-poster bed with chintz curtains, a dressing-table with a muslin flounce round it, and Lorena saw that the room contained all the little luxuries that one of the girls at School had told her were to be found in all large houses which entertained in the proper way.

"You would be surprised, Lorena," she had said, "at the number of things Mama believes are essential to comfort: lots of little satin cushions covered with lace, a writing-table on which there are no less than twenty different items that must be supplied in case a guest wishes to write a letter."

"What can they all be?" Lorena had asked.

"A leather blotter, a box to match to hold writing-paper, a silver ink-stand, a pen-holder, a little pin-cushion, a letter-opener, a calendar, framed lists of the times the posts leave, a pen-tray, a note-book, and lots, lots more which I cannot remember," her friend reeled off.

She took a breath and continued:

"Then of course there must be flowers in the bedroom, carnations or lilies, or orchids if the guest is very grand."

Lorena had laughed at the idea of flowers being chosen according to one's social status.

She noticed that there were lilies in her room and wondered if they were one step up from roses, or perhaps a step below carnations.

She was nearly ready for dinner when there was a knock on the door, and the maid who was help-ing her to dress opened it.

She brought in a tray on which were arranged a number of corsages of different varieties of flowers.

"Will you choose, Miss, which you would like to wear?" she asked.

"What a lovely idea!" Lorena exclaimed. "Do all the Duke's guests have a choice like this?"

"Yes, of course, Miss," the maid replied, "and the gentlemen are offered carnations or gardenias for button-holes."

Lorena found herself hesitating between a corsage of gardenias and another of small star-shaped orchids.

"Which shall I choose?" she asked the maid.

"I think the orchids, Miss. If you like, I'll arrange them in your hair."

"What a good idea!" Lorena smiled. "And thank you for helping me."

As she had no jewellery, she thought the orchids were very decorative, and she hoped that her uncle would think they made her look smarter than she would have looked without them.

Her best evening-gown was one that had been made for her by a dressmaker in Rome whom she preferred to those patronised by the other girls of her age.

Her uncle had given her quite a generous allowance to spend, a gesture, although she did not know it, to placate his conscience when she wrote a little wistfully that most of the girls were going home for the holidays while she was to stay at School.

Because Lorena loved the beautiful paintings that she could see in Rome and appreciated the drapery of the ancient statuary, she preferred al-

most classical clothes to the more elaborate and
fussy creations which were in vogue.

When she looked at the statues of goddesses,
Greek or Roman, that were to be seen everywhere,
she felt that nothing could be more beautiful and
they appealed to her senses in a way she found
hard to describe because to look at them was
somehow an emotional experience.

So Lorena chose to have her gowns made in
white or pure colours and to adapt the fashion so
that there was something classical in every line, in
every draped bodice and softly falling skirt.

Now when she looked at herself in the mirror,
wearing a white gown, she wondered if she had
been right and if her uncle would be disappointed
in her.

"You look very lovely, if I may say so, Miss!"
the maid exclaimed.

"Thank you," Lorena replied. "I am just hoping
I will not look out-of-place in the grandeur of this
magnificent house."

Then she gave a little laugh.

"There is one consolation—nobody is likely to
notice me when there are so many other things to
look at!"

The maid had no time to reply, for at that moment Sir Hugo knocked on the door.

"May I come in?" he enquired.

"Yes, of course, Uncle Hugo, I am quite ready."

She ran towards him, and when he saw the white
orchids in her hair he smiled.

"I was wondering which flowers you would
choose," he said.

"It was quite a difficult choice," Lorena replied,

"but Emily has helped me. She has been very kind in looking after me, Uncle Hugo."

"I am glad about that," Sir Hugo said.

He nodded to the maid, who bobbed him a respectful curtsey as he and Lorena left the room.

"Is there anybody I ought to greet in a different way from the others?" Lorena asked as she and Sir Hugo walked down the stairs.

"What do you mean by that?" he enquired.

"I know that one curtseys to Royalty," Lorena replied, "and when a Cardinal came to the Convent we all had to genuflect and kiss his ring."

Sir Hugo smiled.

"I promise you there will be no Cardinals here tonight, nor, as it happens, is there anyone of Royal blood, although it is quite a frequent occurrence for the Duke to have either a member of our Royal Family or one from another country staying in his house."

"If I meet a Royal Prince it will make it more like a fairy-story than ever!" Lorena said.

"Wait until you see the Duke," Sir Hugo replied.

He entered the Blue Drawing-Room and as he did so he was conscious that there was a sudden hush amongst the crowd of people congregated at the far end of the room.

With the artistry of a showman he had deliberately waited until he thought the majority of the guests would be downstairs before he brought Lorena down to meet them.

He was not quite certain what they would think of her unusual appearance, and her gown had certainly surprised him.

At the same time, he had known from years of experience that there was a rightness about it which could not have been improved upon by Worth himself.

The softly draped bodice, the small waist with its wide sash, and the skirt caught up in the front so that it fell into classical folds below her slim hips were a perfect frame for the delicacy of her face and features and the translucent whiteness of her skin.

Whether it was by design or by chance, the only touch of colour about Lorena was the strange blue of her eyes, and there was in fact a faint smile of triumph on Sir Hugo's lips as they walked towards their host.

He knew that every man in the room was staring at Lorena critically.

The women, who had not been let into the secret of the wager, were interested in her as a new arrival only because she was his niece.

He had deliberately asked the Duke not to pay Lorena more attention than he would ordinarily have given to any new arrival.

"If you make the child seem of the least importance," he had said, "you know as well as I do that the women will be down on her like a ton of bricks."

"I will try to ensure you are not handicapped in that way at any rate," the Duke remarked.

"In this instance I am not worrying about myself so much as about Lorena," Sir Hugo replied. "Kitty has already insisted that I find a relative of some sort to take her off our hands, and quite frankly, her time at Mere will decide which one, although, as it happens, the choice is not wide."

"I never would have thought of finding you short

of anything, least of all relations!" the Duke said
with a laugh.

"I have plenty of them, but they are either too
old, too impoverished, or too egotistical to want to
be encumbered with a young girl."

"That last objection might apply to you yourself," the Duke replied, "and if you want the truth,
I think it is rather selfish of Kitty not to give the
child a chance."

"That is exactly what I said," Sir Hugo agreed.
"I thought we would keep her for a Season and try
to get her married off, but Kitty has refused cate-
gorically."

There was a note in Sir Hugo's voice which told
the Duke that it had been a bone of contention
between them.

'It is a pity,' he had thought, 'that Hugo has no
children of his own.'

He was the sort of man who would have liked to
have a son at Eton who would follow in his footsteps by serving in the Life Guards.

Then he remembered that people might think
the same about himself, and determined not to
pursue the subject.

"Let us hope," he said now, "that your niece's
first taste of caviare and champagne does not make
it very difficult for her later to settle down to tea
and buns, or whatever your relations are prepared
to offer her."

"That is exactly what it will be," Sir Hugo replied, "tea and buns, and doubtless eaten in a
Vicarage."

As he spoke he remembered that a Vicarage had
been Lorena's home, and he thought he should
not have expected her to be anything but a rather

parochial young woman, doubtless given to "good works."

Then he remembered that although his brother might have been unworldly he had been very intelligent, and his wife had been the same.

He found it hard to remember very clearly what his sister-in-law had looked like because he had not seen her often.

She had in fact, he was sure, a sweet face, and when he went to her funeral everybody he had spoken to had told him how much she would be missed, and there had been no doubt of the sincerity in their voices or of the tears in their eyes.

Now, he told himself, Lorena was different in every way from what anyone might have expected, even himself.

Aloud he said to her:

"First I must present you to your host, who has been kind enough to invite you to join his party. Alstone, this is my niece, Lorena—the Duke of Windlemere!"

Because he looked so magnificent, so imposing, and so exactly, Lorena told herself, the way a Duke should look, she bobbed him a little curtsey in the same way that the girls at School had always greeted the Mother Superior.

As his hand took hers, she said:

"Thank you so very much for having me here. It is the marvellous, magnificent house I have dreamt about but never expected to see."

"I am gratified that Mere should have been in your dreams," the Duke said.

"And the next thing she will say is that you were in them too!" a woman's voice interposed.

It was Daisy Hellingford who had spoken, and Sir Hugo said:

"This is my niece, Daisy. She has just returned from Rome, where she has been at School."

He turned to Lorena.

"I do not need to tell you that the Countess of Hellingford is known as being one of the most beautiful women in England."

"That is what Alstone should be saying—not you!" Daisy retorted before Lorena could speak.

There was something fantastic about her green gown, which was extremely décolleté, the huge necklace of emeralds round her neck, and the bandeau of the same stones on her head.

Because she was fashionably tall she seemed to tower over Lorena, but as Sir Hugo drew his niece away to introduce her to the other guests, he thought that she did not seem overawed, but merely excited and interested.

To Lorena it seemed as if every man she spoke to was having a secret joke about something with her uncle.

She had no idea what it could be, she only felt rather than heard that it was there in what they said and the way they looked at her.

In some manner she could not explain, it seemed to signify their approval of something he had done, but she did not know what it was.

When dinner was announced, the Duke proceeded in first, with Lady Hellingford on his arm, and a man called Lord Carnforth told Lorena he was to take her in to dinner.

As they walked down the wide passage which led to the Dining-Room, Lorena asked:

"Do you know this house well?"

"Very well," Lord Carnforth replied. "I stay here as frequently as your uncle does."

"And does it seem just as exciting to you now as it did the first time you ever came here?"

"That was a long time ago," Lord Carnforth said. "I have almost forgotten my special feelings at that time. I do, of course, still think it is one of the finest houses in England, which indeed it is!"

"That is what I thought you would say," Lorena answered. "And I want to remember exactly what I feel every moment I am here."

"Why?"

"So that if I never come here again I shall always remember it, and I must not miss anything of what to me is a wonderful and exciting adventure."

Chapter Three

The Duke at dinner had placed the Countess on his left and the Marchioness of Trumpington on his right.

As he wanted to watch Lorena, he had seated her as the next lady beyond the Countess so that he could both see and hear her.

He had been rather surprised at her appearance, because despite her youth she looked distinctive. Although he noticed the simplicity of her inexpensive dress, like her uncle he realised that it had an individuality which made it completely and absolutely right for her.

He imagined that somebody must have helped her choose it.

Doubtless in Rome there were dressmakers who had a true artistic sense, not like those in London who followed the fashion blindly, without taking into consideration the different appearances of their clients.

Looking down the table laden with gold ornaments, the white table-cloth decorated at the sides with wreaths of smilax and in the centre a profusion of purple orchids, the Duke thought that it would be difficult not to notice Lorena.

Her youth and her plain white gown seemed to stand out so that if it had been a Stage-set she would have been the star on whom the audience's attention was focussed while everybody else faded into the background.

It was just a passing thought and he told himself cynically that he must be getting to the age where youth had an attraction of its own.

Then he thought angrily that he was not old enough yet to be looking back into the past, and for a few minutes he responded in a gratifying manner to the blandishments of Daisy Hellingford.

Then once again he found his eyes drawn back to Lorena, and told himself it was because he was the Judge in a contention in which a great deal of money was involved.

She was listening to Lord Carnforth with what he thought was an almost rapt attention, and as Daisy lowered her voice and said something especially for his ears, he could hear Archie holding forth on the merits of his race-horses.

It was a subject on which he was always pleased
to discourse, and the Duke thought it was rather
clever of Lorena to have started him off on it so
early in the evening.

He did not know that Lorena had remembered
that once when her mother had been reading out
to her father the names of the guests at a very
smart party at which his brother had been present,
he had remarked:

"I remember Carnforth as a young boy coming
to stay at home. I did not realise then, of course,
that he would be so successful as to win the
Derby."

"I would love to go to the Derby, Papa!" Lorena
had exclaimed.

Her father had looked at her in surprise.

"Why?" he asked.

"I saw a reproduction of a fantastic painting by
William Frith," she replied, "and it told me that
the Derby must be a wonderful sight."

Her father smiled.

"It is," he said. "I remember going there when I
was at Oxford, and the crowds on the Heath, the
gypsies, and the coaches remain in my mind long
after the race itself."

"That is what to me would be so fascinating,"
Lorena said, "and I am sure your friend must have
been very proud when he won the most famous
race in the world."

"Who told you it was that?" her father asked in
an amused voice.

"That was the description I read in *The Times*."

"One day I hope you will see a Derby," her
father said lightly. "But it seems at the moment
very unlikely that I shall ever do so again."

This had been a casual conversation, but when Lord Carnforth escorted her in to dinner Lorena had remembered, and she reminded him of how he had stayed with her grandfather.

"Good Heavens! That was a long time ago!" he said. "It was soon after I met your uncle, and as he was in his last year at Oxford and I in my first, I was extremely flattered when he asked me to stay."

"And you have been close friends ever since," Lorena said.

"I suppose one might say so," Lord Carnforth replied, remembering how often he disagreed with Sir Hugo.

"Did you have a horse running in the Derby this year?" Lorena asked.

"As a matter of fact I did," he replied, "but he was unplaced. I had hopes for him, only to be disappointed."

"What happened?" Lorena asked sympathetically.

Immediately Lord Carnforth was off, telling her about his horses, about his special methods of training them, and how he was usually right in predicting exactly how they would run and where they would be placed.

If he had been speaking to one of the other ladies they would doubtless have found the subject, which was all too familiar, extremely boring.

But to Lorena it was new, and as she gave Lord Carnforth her full attention she realised that this was not only the greatest interest he had but was also undoubtedly the love of his life.

He paused for a moment, and she asked:

"Do you consider that the way you feed your horses is important?"

"Of course it is!" Lord Carnforth exclaimed. "I have gone to a great deal of trouble to study the different ways of feeding race-horses, and I have worked out a method of my own that usually proves extremely successful."

He paused as if for effect, and Lorena said:

"This may sound a strange question, but are you equally particular about the water they drink?"

Lord Carnforth looked at her and raised his eye-brows in surprise.

"I am asking you this," Lorena said, "because in Rome, where if it rains excessively the Tiber floods, there have been reports of a great deal of illness in the lower parts of the city."

She looked at Lord Carnforth to see if he was listening, then went on:

"Although there is anxiety about the effect of bad water on human beings, no-one ever seems to worry about the animals, which surely can be up-set too."

Lord Carnforth looked at her for a moment, then said:

"That is a very interesting theory, which I must say had never struck me. I always take my horses' food anywhere they are racing, but I have never thought of taking the water to which they are ac-customed."

The Duke, who had been listening to the last part of the conversation and ignoring something particularly provocative which the Countess was saying to him, bent forward to remark:

"It never struck me, Archie, that water could be important in the training of horses, but now that I think of it, it appears to be sheer common sense, and what is more, I suspect that the water in some of the stables in which we put our horses before a race is definitely unclean."

"Water varies all over the country..." Lord Carnforth began, then he exclaimed:

"Do you know, I believe this child is right! I remember at a race-meeting three weeks ago noticing that my horses seemed to dislike the water they were being given, and the buckets too were dirty."

"It certainly gives us a new explanation," the Duke said, "as to why horses which seem perfectly fit when they leave home fail in a race when they should, by all statistics, win easily."

Because the Duke was speaking, the men at his end of the table were all listening, and now an argument began, which in a very short time involved the whole table.

There was not a man amongst the Duke's friends who, if he was not an actual race-horse owner, was not deeply interested in the "Sport of Kings."

Now they were all expressing their opinions on what was an entirely new idea.

It was quite a long time and several courses later when the gentleman on Lorena's other side said with a smile:

"You certainly seem to have started something. Who suggested to you in the first place that what they drink might affect the running of horses?"

"When I spoke of water to Lord Carnforth," Lorena replied, "I was actually thinking that if it is polluted or dirty it must affect all animals; and of course in Rome the Nuns always warned us to be careful of what we drank when we went into the city."

"I gather, from that, that your School was outside."

Lorena nodded.

"It was in a very beautiful position with a fine view especially of St. Peter's."

"I have not been to Rome for a long time," her partner said, "but I remember being very impressed with the Colosseum and of course the fountains."

"They are beautiful," Lorena agreed. "I am so lucky to have been educated in a place which makes one want instinctively to learn, and which is so redolent of history."

"I hope you are interested in the present as well as the past," the man beside her remarked, and there was something slightly flirtatious in his voice.

"But of course!" Lorena replied. "And in the ... future."

As she spoke, she remembered that she had no idea what her future would hold.

Just for a moment she looked anxious and glanced at her uncle, who was farther down the table, hoping that he would think she was behaving in the right way and perhaps would not be in too much of a hurry to be rid of her.

"What is worrying you?"

The man on her right was a Major in what had been her uncle's Regiment, the Life Guards, and his name was Kelvin Fane. Although Lorena was not aware of it, he was heir presumptive to a Dukedom.

He was one of the most sought-after men in London, and although he had an extremely able brain and would have done well in politics, he preferred to stay in his Regiment.

Because it was always stationed in London he spent his time flirting with beautiful women, "moving relentlessly," as one wag put it, "from *Boudoir* to *Boudoir!*"

He had never looked at a young and marriageable girl and his only interest in Lorena now was that he had a bet, and quite a considerable one, that Hugo Benson was bound to lose to Lord Carnforth.

Now, watching Lorena, he was not so sure.

He liked the way she spoke, her soft musical voice, her unselfconsciousness, and the manner in which she looked straight into the eyes of the person to whom she was speaking.

She was smiling as she spoke to him now, and he thought that in a few years' time she would be the sort of beauty who would turn men's heads, and it would be a pity if by that time he was too old to pursue her.

While the rest of the guests at the table were still talking about race-horses and water, impulsively, without really considering if he should do so, Major Fane dropped his voice to say:

"And what do you expect to find in the future— love, or marriage?"

"Surely they are synonymous," Lorena replied. "And I suppose that is what I would ... like to find ... eventually."

"Why not at once?"

"Because, while it may sound rather foolish to you, there are so many places I would like to go and so much I want to learn."

She saw that he looked surprised, and she explained:

"I have been at School for the last three years. Rome is beautiful, but the world is very big."

Major Fane laughed at the way she spoke.

"Very big!" he agreed. "But you cannot expect to go exploring by yourself, and if you were married, your husband would doubtless take you to Paris. All pretty women want to go to Paris."

"Why?" Lorena enquired.

"Because it is the city of gaiety and love, and the French know how to accommodate lovers better than any other nation in the world."

"You mean . . . they specialise in it?" Lorena asked. "How strange!"

"Why strange?"

"Because surely everybody, regardless of where they are born, wants to love and be loved. I cannot think why the French should think it is exclusive to their nation."

Major Fane smiled.

"That is a question to which you will know the answer when you are older."

"Perhaps no-one will want to take me to Paris."

The Major laughed.

"I can reassure you by telling you that a great number of men will suggest that very thing, of course after the wedding-ring is on your finger."

There was a touch of cynicism in his voice, and Lorena looked puzzled for a moment before she said:

"Before I go to Paris, there is a great deal in England I want to see, besides other parts of the world."

She gave a little sigh, then went on:

"But I expect most of it will have to remain where it is already—in a book or in my mind. I have no money with which to travel."

"That again can easily be remedied, if you choose a rich husband."

Lorena laughed.

"I arrived back in England from School today, and I think I may have to wait for a long time before anybody asks me to be his wife. Besides, I should want to be very much in love before I accepted."

Major Fane raised his eye-brows.

"Has Kitty heard you talk like this?" he asked.

"No; I have not seen my aunt for three years."

"Then I warn you, if Kitty arranges your marriage she will not consider the dictates of your heart, only the size of the applicant's bank-balance!"

Major Fane was speaking in a manner which would have made the women with whom he usually associated scream with laughter and declare him to be wickedly witty.

But Lorena merely looked worried.

"You are . . . frightening me," she said after a moment. "Although I am sure it is unnecessary, because I decided a long time ago that I would never marry anyone unless I was in love."

Major Fane was just about to tell her that her ideas were not only out-of-date but extremely impracticable in the social life enjoyed by her uncle and aunt.

Then somehow he changed the words he was about to say, and in a very different voice from the one he had used before, he said quietly:

"Then I hope, Miss Benson, you will fall in love

with somebody who loves you, and of course live happily ever after."

He was not being cynical and he spoke with a sincerity that surprised himself.

Instantly the smile was back on Lorena's lips and in her eyes.

"Thank you," she said, "that is just what I would like to hear, especially tonight when I am here."

Major Fane wondered what she meant by that, but before he could ask her for an explanation, the lady on his other side attracted his attention and Lorena turned back to Lord Carnforth.

"Now look what you have done with your revolutionary ideas!" he exclaimed. "You have got everybody arguing. I do not mind telling you that either the Duke or I will bring up this whole subject at the next Jockey Club meeting."

"I do hope I shall be able to hear the result," Lorena said.

"I promise I will tell you what they say," Lord Carnforth replied.

"Thank you. I should like to think of your horses winning every race in which you enter them simply because they were given the right sort of water."

When the ladies left the room, Lord Carnforth moved up to sit next to the Duke, and Sir Hugo came from the other end of the table to sit near them.

"What started that extraordinary argument about water of all things?" he asked. "It is not a liquid I usually associate with a dinner-party at Mere!"

The Duke laughed.

"I should hope not! But it was in fact your niece's idea in the first place."

"Lorena's?" Sir Hugo asked in astonishment. "I do not believe it!"

"It is true," Archie Carnforth said. "I have to admit, Hugo, that she has an original mind, if nothing else."

"I cannot remember when we last had a discussion at dinner which involved every man present," the Duke said.

There was a twist to his lips as he added:

"Daisy informed me that it was the most boring meal she had ever spent in my company."

Sir Hugo looked at him apprehensively.

"For Heaven's sake," he said in a low voice, "do not let Daisy get her knife into Lorena. She dislikes women anyway, and a child straight from School is hardly up to her weight."

"No, indeed," the Duke agreed.

"Nevertheless, it is an extremely interesting idea," Lord Carnforth was saying. "In fact, I am now certain that that was what was wrong with my horse. . . ."

He was off again on the subject of his horses, and the rest of the men who had intended to say something about Lorena found themselves side-tracked into the same argument, until the Duke signalled that it was time to join the ladies.

Both he and Sir Hugo entered the Drawing-Room wondering what they would find.

They were aware that it was a much more demanding test for Lorena to be with the women than with the men.

Sir Hugo half-suspected that he would find his

niece sitting outside the group, feeling rather shy
and possibly tongue-tied.

To his surprise and to the Duke's, she was deep
in conversation with, of all people, The Marchioness
of Trumpington.

Enid Trumpington had been a beauty who had
married a man far older than herself, one who had
given her a social position to which she would not
have been entitled as a young girl.

Beautiful, with red hair and skin that was the
envy of her contemporaries, she was extremely
passionate. Her love-affairs, which followed one
another in quick succession, had given the Social
World something to talk about for the last ten years.

She was at the moment being extremely indis-
creet with Lord Gilmour, who was also a guest at
Mere.

Lord Gilmour had the misfortune of being
married to a woman who was always ill, always
complaining, and preferred to live in the country.

Everybody had been extremely sorry for him, as
he was a man who enjoyed gaiety, good living, and
the company of beautiful women; and when he
first started his *affaire de coeur* with Enid Trumpington, it had been considered quite suitable.

Now they were, as Daisy Hellingford had said
tartly: "making an exhibition of themselves."

In fact, it seemed to everybody that it was only
a question of time before both the Marquis and
Lady Gilmour became aware of what was happening.

The Marquis of Trumpington was getting old,
but he was important in Court circles and because
of his long experience he was still greatly in demand
by the new King.

The fact that he was so often in attendance at Buckingham Palace or Windsor Castle left the Marchioness with a great deal of freedom which she would otherwise not have had, and she and Lord Gilmour made the most of it.

They were, however, overstepping the bounds of behaviour which had been summed up during the last Reign in one very pertinent command: "Thou shalt not cause a scandal!"

There were whispers that Jack Gilmour and Enid Trumpington had been seen alone together in Paris.

And it was all too painfully obvious when they were at parties that they had eyes for no-one but each other.

The Duke, who had had a flirtation with Enid some years earlier, was well aware that her fiery and insatiable nature made it difficult for her to be restrained or discreet.

Yet he thought that Gilmour would have had more sense, and he decided that during this week at Mere he would speak to him and suggest, as a good friend, that he should observe the proprieties more closely.

Things had changed in the last three years, and under the new King and Queen the codes of behaviour had become very much more conventional.

King George and Queen Mary were propriety itself, and although in consequence the Court was much duller and, the Duke thought, very boring, there was no doubt that they were setting new standards which, unless they would invite disaster, must be followed by all those who wished to be accepted in the best Society.

He wondered, as he walked down the length of the long and beautiful room, what Enid Trumpington could possibly have to say to a girl as young as Lorena.

He only hoped that she was not being unpleasant to the child as he and Hugo were afraid Daisy might be.

He would have liked to go up to the Marchioness and find out what she was discussing with Lorena.

Instead, as if in duty bound, he moved to Daisy Hellingford's side.

"Alstone, are we going to play Bridge?" she enquired. "Or perhaps a game of Baccarat would be fun. I am sick to death of horses! I never want to hear of one again!"

"We will do whatever you like," the Duke said good-humouredly. "It shall be Baccarat, if you prefer."

As he spoke, he knew that this meant he would pay any losses that Daisy incurred, while she would keep her winnings.

But if she was amused he was quite prepared to concur.

"It shall be Baccarat," Daisy decided.

She clapped her hands and said in a loud voice:

"Who is prepared to lose a lot of money, because tonight I feel my luck is in!"

There was some laughter and some slightly sarcastic remarks at this, but those who wished to play moved across the Drawing-Room and into the Ante-Room, where gaming-tables of every sort were ready for anyone who felt inclined to use them.

As the Duke had not dared to do, Sir Hugo walked up to the Marchioness of Trumpington to say:

"I can see you are being very kind, Enid, to my niece. I am grateful, because I am sure you are aware it must be quite an ordeal to arrive here as she has, knowing only one person, and that, her uncle."

"A very attractive uncle, which of course makes a difference," the Marchioness replied, who could never resist flattering any man whether she was interested in him or not.

"Thank you, Enid. May I say how lovely you look tonight, although it is not surprising."

The Marchioness smiled and rose to her feet.

"I must go and play with Jack," she said, "otherwise he will lose to Daisy every penny he possesses, which is something I have no intention of allowing."

She paused for a moment before she moved away, to say to Lorena:

"You and I, dear, must have another talk again soon."

Lorena had stood up politely when the Marchioness did, and now Sir Hugo sat down in the chair she had vacated and asked:

"What were you talking about?"

"She was telling me how she felt and what she did when she was my age."

Sir Hugo looked surprised, but before he could ask more, Major Fane came towards them and said:

"I am sure there is something quite wrong in an uncle and niece sitting together. It is almost as bad as one of those official dinners where a man has always to sit beside his wife."

"If by that you mean to talk to Lorena," Sir Hugo said, "I am delighted to concede that you have a prior claim, as you sat next to her at dinner."

"I was going to suggest," Major Fane said, "that she might like to watch the gambling. What takes place at Mere is quite an education in itself."

"It is very kind of you," Lorena said, "and it is something I would . . . like to do. But first, would it be very rude if I . . . looked at the paintings . . . in this room?"

She spoke a little hesitatingly and looked at Sir Hugo as she spoke, as if she feared he might think it incorrect.

But her uncle merely smiled.

"It is rather clever of you, as it happens," he said, "for Major Fane will inherit one of the finest collections of paintings in the country, and there is no-one who knows more about them."

As Lorena rose eagerly from the chair in which she was sitting, he added:

"He is a walking guide-book, so make the most of it while you have the opportunity."

"I shall!" Lorena said so fervently that both her uncle and Major Fane laughed.

*   *   *

Lorena awoke and thought with delight that it was morning.

She told herself last night when she went to bed, very late by Convent standards, that she begrudged every moment that she must waste in sleeping when there were so many fascinating and exciting things to see and do at Mere.

"There are no plans for tomorrow," the Duke had said before they went up to bed, "and most of you have been here often enough to know that everything I own is at your disposal, and you have only to ask for anything you want."

Because there were expressions of surprise on the faces of some of his guests, he explained:

"I am saying this because there is somebody here

who has never stayed at Mere before, but doubtless
her uncle had told her what to expect."

"I have hardly had time," Sir Hugo protested,
"so you tell her, Alstone. It comes much better from
you."

"Very well," the Duke said, and turned to Lorena
to say:

"As everybody else knows, there is tennis, croquet,
golf, horses to ride if you prefer them, and punts
on the lake, although I beg you not to trust yourself
to Fane, who got stuck in the mud last time he
attempted to squire a lovely lady!"

"That was *his* story!" somebody said, laughing.
"And Miss Benson is too young to be allowed in a
punt alone with Kelvin!"

There was more laughter at that.

The Duke thought Lorena looked a little shy,
and he went on:

"There are not only horses in the stables to ride,
but you can be driven anywhere you wish, or, if you
prefer, there are cars at your disposal. I suppose
there are other things, but I cannot think of them at
the moment."

"Kelvin will fill in the gaps very eloquently," one
man teased.

Lorena wondered why there were so many jokes
about Major Fane.

He had been so kind in showing her the paintings
not only in the Drawing-Room but in several of the
other rooms as well.

There had been some laughing remarks she had
not understood when they had returned to the Blue
Drawing-Room, and she had thought that the
Viscountess of Storr had spoken to the Major in
rather a sharp manner.

Lorene had not noticed her before, but she was a tall, dark, attractive woman with a deep, slow voice which reminded Lorena of a purring cat.

She had looked across at the Major when they reappeared and said:

"I never imagined cradle-snatching was particularly in your line, Kelvin!"

"But paintings are, Sarah," he answered, "and Sir Hugo asked me to show them to his niece."

The Viscountess had shrugged her shoulders and walked away in a manner which Lorena knew showed that she was angry.

Because she thought it must have been her fault for keeping the Major so long out of the Drawing-Room, she was just about to apologise, when the Duke joined them.

"You enjoyed seeing my paintings?" he asked.

"You have a very beautiful collection," she replied, "far better than anything I have seen in Rome. But then I have always preferred the English artists, and your Constables are magnificent!"

The Duke looked at her in surprise, and Major Fane with a twinkle in his eyes said:

"You will find Miss Benson knows a great deal about paintings."

He moved away as he spoke, and Lorena said:

"I wanted to . . . thank him."

"You will have plenty of time to do that," the Duke said. "Now tell me, which of my paintings that you have seen so far is your favourite?"

He thought that like most people who visited Mere she would find it almost impossible to pick out anything in particular, but instead she answered without hesitation:

"The Romneys, but that is not only because of the artist but the subject."

"You mean those he painted of Emma Hamilton?" the Duke enquired.

"Yes."

"You admire the redoubtable Lady Hamilton?"

"I admire her because she not only educated and improved herself until she could entertain the most important people in Naples, including the King and Queen," Lorena answered, "but she also inspired the greatest sailor England has ever known."

She spoke with such enthusiasm that the Duke was amused.

"Are you really condoning an illicit love-affair?" he asked. "Surely you remember that Lady Hamilton had a husband and Lord Nelson had a wife?"

There was a pause for a moment and he saw the colour rise faintly in Lorena's cheeks.

"I had not really ... thought of it ... like that," she said. "I was remembering how she persuaded the King of Naples to allow the British Fleet to water in their Ports when at first the Napolese had refused because they were frightened of Napoleon."

She paused for a moment before she added:

"If they had not been able to do that, there would never have been the Battle of the Nile, when Napoleon's Fleet was completely annihilated."

"I am recalling my history now," the Duke said, "but I am still interested that a woman who was in love with a man who was not her husband should command your admiration."

"I think perhaps ... that part of the story was rather ... glossed over in our history-books," Lorena said a little hesitatingly, "but helping and inspiring Lord Nelson could not be ... wrong. And if it was activated by love, then we must forgive her, considering how much she did for England."

The Duke was rather intrigued.

He had somehow expected that a girl coming from a Convent, and certainly one so young, would have been shocked and even horrified by anything that concerned an illicit liaison.

But from what Lorena had said he was quite certain that she did not understand the full story of Emma Hamilton's wild infatuation for Lord Nelson and his for her.

But she was certainly not condemning, as he had thought she would, a married woman who had loved another man.

He wondered what Lorena would say if she knew of the intrigues and affairs that were taking place at Mere at this particular moment.

There was not one man in the party, with the exception of Sir Hugo, who was not involved with one of the women present.

Hugo Benson was, to the Duke's knowledge, captivated by an extremely attractive lady. But he had deliberately not invited her to Mere. To make the numbers right, Hugo had to partner Lorena.

Also the Duke was certain, from all he knew of young girls, which was very little, that Lorena would be shocked if she had any idea that there was anything irregular in her uncle and aunt's relationship.

The whole of the Windlemere Set were aware that Hugo and Kitty had not been getting on, both having had separate interests for some years, but as that was nothing unusual and applied to almost every other married couple, it had long ago ceased to be a subject of any interest.

Now the Duke said:

"I hope tomorrow, or at least while you are staying here, you will look at my Romneys with me. I shall be interested to hear more of your comments on the beautiful Emma."

Lorena appeared to be thinking for a moment, then she said:

"There is so much I want to see, so much I would like to know and learn about the treasures you have here. Surely you have a Curator who would not mind answering my questions?"

"I have one, but I am perfectly prepared to answer your questions myself."

"I am sure you would find all I want to know tedious, even if you had the time," Lorena said.

She was not speaking flirtatiously as any other woman might have done, waiting for the Duke to assure her that he would always have the time where she was concerned. She was just stating a fact, and she was obviously anxious not to be a nuisance.

"I am perfectly willing to be a most informative guide," the Duke said, "but in case I am not available, you will find my Curator, Mr. Ashley, very knowledgeable, and any of the servants will take you to his office."

"Thank you."

"Do you intend to spend all tomorrow sight-seeing?"

"Not all day," Lorena replied. "You did say your guests could ride. Since Uncle Hugo was kind enough to pay for the lessons, I have been riding in Rome, but the horses there were very docile."

"I can assure you that mine are quite the opposite," the Duke said.

"That is what I was hoping," Lorena replied, smiling.

She remembered the conversation now, and decided that early in the morning would be a good time to go riding, before anybody was about.

She jumped out of bed and went to the window to pull back the curtains.

It was very early and the mist which still lay over the lake swirled round the trunks of the trees on the other side of it.

The sun, however, was rapidly dispersing it and giving the garden and everything she could see a kind of golden glow.

Lorena made a little sound of sheer delight and began to dress herself.

She had a riding-habit which, although it was not very smart, had been made in England and was therefore well cut.

She struggled into it, thinking that although it was shabby because she had had it before she went to Italy, it was unlikely that anyone would see her and therefore it would not really matter.

She glanced at the clock on the mantelpiece and saw that it was only five-thirty, and, being sure that she could ride unseen, she decided not to wear a hat.

She arranged her hair simply and with plenty of hair-pins so that it should not become untidy, took a last quick glance at herself in the mirror, and opened her bedroom door and went very quietly down the stairs.

As she expected, the front door was open and the steps were being scrubbed by two maids in mob-caps.

There were also a number of footmen without

their powdered wigs and liveried coats, hurrying about in their shirt-sleeves and crested-buttoned waist-coats.

They looked at Lorena in surprise, but she merely said: "Good-morning!" and hurried out through the front door to turn towards the stables.

She knew where they were, for her uncle had pointed them out yesterday afternoon as they had driven down the oak-bordered drive that led up to the house.

"The stables are older than the Robert Adam building," he had said, "and they are believed to be the finest in the country, but I suspect you will be more interested in what they contain."

Lorena thought now she was interested in both, and was only hoping that she was not so early that the grooms would still be asleep.

But as she went through the arch which led to the stables, she saw the horses with their heads over the open half-doors of their stalls and a number of stable-lads carrying water-buckets and bales of hay.

She stopped the first one she came to.

"Good-morning! His Grace said I could ride. I wonder if somebody could saddle me a horse?"

"Yus o' course, Ma'am," the boy answered.

He put down his bucket and went through an open door and Lorena followed him.

She found that in this part of the stable the stalls did not look out onto the yard, and as she went down the passage she looked at the horses, thinking each one finer than the last.

"Good-mornin'!" said a respectful voice beside her, and she looked round to find an elderly groom. "Oi understands ye wish ter ride, Ma'am."

"Yes, please," Lorena answered.

"Som'n quiet, mebbe?"

"Not too quiet!"

"Oi got jus' the roight mount for a lady," the groom said, smiling. "This one 'ere."

He stepped into one of the stalls, and as he did so, Lorena saw a large stallion in the next stall which a groom was saddling.

As if without asking the question the groom was aware of her curiosity, he said:

"That be fer 'is Grace, Ma'am. Oi 'spects as ye're up so early, ye'll be a-riding wi' 'im."

"I had no idea he would be riding so early," Lorena answered, "but I would like to do so, if he would not feel it was an intrusion."

"Not 'im Ma'am!" the groom replied. "Th' truth be that 'is Grace is so energetic 'e's up afore anyone else in t' house 'as their eyes open."

He gave a chuckle as he said:

"It'll be a surprise to 'is Grace to see ye 'ere so broight and early."

He was right, Lorena thought, as a few minutes later she followed the groom as he led the horse round to the front door for the Duke.

The Duke was already there waiting, and, she noticed, looking extremely smart in his breeches and highly polished boots, and wearing a whip-cord riding-jacket which had obviously been cut by a master-hand.

His tall hat was on the side of his dark head and he carried a crop.

There was no mistaking his astonishment as he saw Lorena.

"You are up very early, Miss Benson!" he exclaimed.

"I thought I would be the only person who would wish to ride before breakfast," Lorena answered. "But if you would rather be alone, I can easily ride by myself."

"I would not be so ungallant as to suggest such an idea!" the Duke replied. "We will ride together, and I only hope, after all you said, that my horse is spirited enough for you."

"I shall be very embarrassed if he is too spirited and throws me off or I cannot control him," Lorena replied with a smile.

The Duke mounted the stallion that was being held for him.

"That is something we shall have to prove," he said, and they set off side-by-side.

Then as they crossed the bridge that spanned the lake, the Duke asked almost automatically:

"Are you all right?"

"I was just thinking," Lorena answered, "that I definitely am dreaming. I am riding a magnificent horse and I am staying in the most magificent house I have ever seen! I do hope I shall not wake up too quickly."

The Duke laughed.

"I hope so too. But surely there is someone in your dream you have omitted to mention?"

For a moment Lorena did not understand, then she smiled.

"If you mean you," she said, "of course you are magnificent too! Mr. Gillingham said you were Prince Charming, and I am sure you are aware that that is exactly who you are."

She spoke naturally, without any touch of self-consciousness, and the Duke thought a little wryly that it was not the sort of compliment to which he was used; in fact, he was not certain if it was a compliment at all.

Then he was aware that Lorena was no longer thinking of him but concentrating on her riding and, he sensed, longing to gallop as soon as they were clear of the trees.

"She is certainly unpredictable," he told himself, and settled down to follow her as she forged ahead.

Chapter Four

Driving to Church, the Duke found himself thinking about Lorena.

It was only a short distance, and it was a tradition that in the winter he drove in his closed Brougham and in the summer in an open Victoria, as his father and mother had always done.

If he had suggested going by car, he was quite certain there would have been a revolution amongst the old servants.

When Robert Adam had built Mere on the site of an older house, he had not, as was usual for the period, included a private Chapel, because there was already a very beautiful Norman Church just inside the Park.

It was part of the history of the family, and the elaborate tombs, added to down the centuries, enriched the ancient building.

It was the Duke's father who had decided that the whole household must attend Church on Sundays and that the Service should be at seven-thirty in the morning, which would entail less inconvenience than if it was held at a later hour.

Accordingly, a long line of servants walked the quarter-of-a-mile down the drive to the Church, headed by the butler and Mrs. Kingston and fol-

lowed by the other servants in order of seniority
down to the youngest and most newly joined knife-
boy.

The Duke habitually arrived at two minutes to
the half-hour, and he would have been extremely
annoyed if, owing to any oversight by his valet or
lack of punctuality on the part of his coachman,
he was even a quarter-of-a-minute late.

It was when the Victoria crossed over the bridge
that he found himself regretting that this morning
he would miss his ride and be unable to accompany
Lorena as he had done yesterday.

He was quite certain that she would take the
opportunity of riding one of his horses again.

It had given her such pleasure that when they
had finished their first gallop he had seen her eyes
were shining like stars, and her whole face seemed
to have lit up as a child's might have done at some
unexpected treat.

Yesterday they had ridden for very nearly three-
quarters-of-an-hour before the Duke said:

"It is now nearly half-past-six. Are you feeling
hungry?"

"Now that you mention it, I am!" Lorena replied.
"I was too excited to eat very much dinner last
night, delicious though it was."

"Then I think you are entitled to a good breakfast. Follow me."

He rode on ahead before she could reply, and a
few minutes later she saw in front of her an old
and very attractive farm-house.

It had in fact stood on the Estate for many
centuries, and was built of red brick and ships'
timbers and its gabled roof and twisted chimneys
were a complement to its diamond-paned casements.

Despite its picturesque appearance, it was, however, a farm-house, with cocks and hens pecking pieces of grain in a yard at the side of it, a number of cows with their calves in a field at the back, and on the pond which was bordered by yellow king-cups were dozens of fat white ducks.

"It is the prettiest farm I have ever seen!" Lorena exclaimed.

After a farm-lad had taken their horses from them they had walked into a large flagged kitchen with hams hung from the low beams, and the farmer's wife came hurrying to greet them as she wiped her hands on her apron.

"Good-mornin', Your Grace," she said to the Duke, dropping a curtsey. "It's real nice to see ye! When I heard ye were up at the big house I was a-hoping ye'd call in on us."

"I am not only feeling hungry for one of your excellent breakfasts, Mrs. Swallow," the Duke replied, "but I have brought a guest who I know will find your eggs and ham as delicious as I do."

"Ye be very welcome," Mrs. Swallow said to Lorena.

She led the way across the kitchen and into what she called "the Parlour."

It was a somewhat stiff room, with an upright piano, framed texts embroidered in wool on the walls, and a bow-fronted window which had a view over the undulating green meadows to the distant hills, which made Lorena exclaim with delight.

"I always say that Hundle Farm has a better view than I have at Mere," the Duke said.

"It is lovely!" Lorena exclaimed. "But so far I have found nothing amongst your possesssions that is anything else."

"That is what I like to hear," the Duke said complacently.

He sat down at the round table that was set in the window, and when Mrs. Swallow had covered it with a white cloth she brought in all the things which Lorena associated with a farm.

A cottage loaf, hot and crisp from the oven, a huge pat of golden butter, a comb of honey which came from the hives she could see in the field outside, and a few minutes later a big plate of eggs with slices of ham.

"It's fortunate, Your Grace, that us have a ham just ready to eat," Mrs. Swallow said.

"I am hoping I may have another of your hams up at the house," the Duke said. "There is no-one in the whole district, as you well know, Mrs. Swallow, who can cure a ham as well as you."

"'Tis a secret as has been handed down from me great-grandmother," Mrs. Swallow replied. "And it be nice to know Your Grace appreciates it."

"I do indeed," the Duke answered.

Anticipating what he might require when he had finished the eggs, Mrs. Swallow brought in a newly carved cold ham, which, when Lorena had eaten a few slices, she thought was more delicious than any ham she had ever tasted before.

She then ate a slice of the hot bread, spreading it with butter and honey, and only when she saw the Duke smiling as she helped herself to another slice did she say:

"I am afraid I am being rather . . . greedy."

"I am glad you are young enough to enjoy simple things, like a farm breakfast," the Duke said.

"It is delicious! Do you always come here when you go riding?"

"When I am alone."

"But you brought me."

"As I have said, I thought you would enjoy a farm breakfast, while most of the ladies who stay at Mere only toy with a cup of coffee."

"I hope I shall never get like that."

"Are you anticipating that you might?" the Duke asked.

"I am afraid that Uncle Hugo and Aunt Kitty, if I stay with them, will want me to behave in a fashionable manner ... but acutally I think they will send me ... away, to live with one of my ... other relations."

There was no doubt that the idea was worrying her, and the Duke said after a moment:

"Your aunt is very fond of London. Is that what you would enjoy?"

"I think it would be unfair if I said no, because I have never been to parties, but what I would really like would be to live in the country, with horses to ride ... and perhaps have a few real friends ... not a whole ... crowd of ... acquaintances."

Lorena spoke slowly and seriously, as if she was thinking out what she was saying; then before the Duke could reply, she looked out the window and said:

"I think farmers are very lucky people because they must feel like God."

"Like God?" the Duke repeated. "What do you mean by that?"

Lorena gave him a little smile that was almost apologetic.

"It came into my mind, when I saw the calves and the lambs, the chickens and the piglets, that farmers are always creating new life. Every year young animals are born, and that in itself must not only be exciting but must give them a feeling of omnipotence."

The Duke laughed.

"I have never heard that idea before. You certainly seem to be full of originality."

Lorena glanced at him quickly as if she thought she might have said something wrong, and without her having to ask the question, the Duke said:

"Originality is what most people lack. I am just wondering where those ideas of yours come from."

"Out of my head," Lorena replied disarmingly.

"And with whom have you discussed them before?"

"Not many people," she replied. "The girls at School wanted to talk about the things they had done in the holidays, and as I never came home, I could not join in with them in that! Otherwise they talked about what they were going to do when they left School, and I had no idea what would happen to me."

"Are you telling me that you talk to yourself?" the Duke asked.

"Not really." Lorena smiled. "I think to myself and make up stories, but I never dreamt that I would ever see a house as magnificent as yours and have the opportunity to see the treasures it contains. Yours at Mere are fantastic!"

"You have not yet seen all of them."

"Perhaps ... there will not be ... time to see the ... rest."

She gave a little sigh and added:

"I do hope Uncle Hugo will not want to ... leave until I have ... seen everything."

"Let me reassure you by saying that as far as I know, your uncle is quite prepared to stay for nearly a week."

"That is what I hoped," Lorena said, "and thank you, thank you, thank you very much for having me here!"

"If I say it is a pleasure," the Duke said, "that will sound rather trite, the polite remark one always makes, but actually on this occasion it is the truth."

She gave him a smile as if he had given her a very special present, then helped herself to another slice of bread.

'She is completely natural,' the Duke thought now as the carriage proceeded down the drive towards the Church.

He remembered how as they rode home, when Mere came in sight Lorena had said:

"I suppose we . . . have to go . . . back? I would like to go on riding for . . . hours and hours, and . . . miles and miles."

"There are other days for you to ride."

"Yes, I know," Lorena replied, "but I wish, just the same . . . sometimes that time . . . could stand . . . still."

There was something in her voice that made him ask:

"I wonder if you are telling me in a rather roundabout way that you have been a little apprehensive or shy of meeting all the people who are staying with me?"

It would have been, he thought as he spoke, understandable for any young girl to feel like that, and it was what they had all expected of Lorena before she had arrived.

And yet she had not behaved at all in the way that Archie Carnforth had said she would.

She answered:

"Mama always used to say that being shy was a form of selfishness; one was thinking about oneself instead of other people."

"But surely," the Duke insisted, "you were just a little shy when you first arrived?"

"There did seem to be a number of ... butterflies fluttering ... inside me," Lorena confessed, "but when I saw . . . you, I forgot about . . . myself."

"Why me?" the Duke enquired.

"Because you were exactly what I had hoped the owner of my dream-house would look like, and Mr. Gillingham had said Mere was like a Fairy-Palace."

"I am glad I did not disappoint you."

"No, you were just right, and so was everybody else—the beautiful ladies glittering with jewels and moving as gracefully as swans in their evening-gowns, the flowers on the table at dinner, the paintings, the gold ornaments—I shall always remember it!"

Now, thinking over what she had said, the Duke thought to himself that she was seeing everything as if it were a painting, and perceptively he guessed that neither he nor the rest of the party was to her really human.

Lorena was a child watching a play upon a Stage, entranced, absorbed in what she saw and heard, but not feeling that it was in any way personal or that she was actually part of it.

He did not know why he understood that, he only felt as if in some way he could read her thoughts and sense the feeling she had tried to put into words.

With a little start he realised that the carriage had reached the Church.

He could see the Vicar in his white surplice waiting in the porch to receive him and escort him up the aisle to the huge carved family pew which was situated in the Chancel.

He stepped out of the carriage and held out his hand.

"Good-morning, Vicar!"

"Good-morning, Your Grace! It is a great honour to have you worship with us once again."

These formal words were always spoken on such occasions, and without waiting for the Duke's reply the Vicar went ahead and they were led by the Verger up the aisle between the pews, which were packed with the servants from Mere and a few of the villagers.

Because he had been thinking of Lorena, the Duke was not really surprised to find her already in the family pew.

As the Vicar showed him into the special seat carved with his coat-of-arms and he sat down on the red velvet cushions, he saw that Lorena, with her head tipped upwards, was looking at the beautiful stained-glass window above the altar.

She was wearing a thin muslin gown, for although it was early in the morning it was already quite hot. On her head was the turned-back hat in which she had travelled, and which gave her a very young appearance and looked somewhat like a halo.

She did not look at the Duke, and, wondering if she was really aware of his presence, he thought again how unpredictable she was.

He could not imagine being alone, even in a Church, with any other woman and not find her flashing, meaningful glances of intimacy and managing even in such a sanctified place to make him aware not only of her femininity but also her interest in him personally.

The Service began, and the organ, which had been a present to the Church from the Duke's mother, was played surprisingly well by a resident of the village.

The Choir consisted mainly of School-children who were forced to attend, and they sang the psalms and the hymns more musically than one would have expected in a small village Church.

Once again it had been the Duke's mother, who had been musical, who had taken a great deal of trouble to see that the Choir was well trained and the Choir-Master was paid for his services.

As Lorena had been at a Catholic Convent, the Duke wondered if she would have difficulty finding her way through the English prayer-book. But as she appeared to be very at home with it, he decided that she had doubtless attended the British Embassy Church in Rome.

He could hear her joining in the psalms and hymns in a clear young voice which he was sure would have delighted his mother.

The Service was short, which again was traditional, for the last Duke had insisted that no sermon should last more than ten minutes.

If it went on any longer, he would look at his watch and walk out.

The Vicar was therefore careful to keep within the time-limit, and the Duke was aware that Lorena listened all the time he was speaking and did not fidget.

If there was one thing the Duke disliked it was a woman who fidgeted all the time, and he found Daisy Hellingford's habit of playing with her pearls and twiddling her rings round her fingers increasingly irritating.

"Do you not realise," he had asked her once, "that when you are always moving unnecessarily, you dissipate your energy? I was reading an article by a Doctor on that subject only the other day."

"I have all the energy left that you need, dearest Alstone," Daisy had replied, "and sometimes a surplus which is wasted."

There was no mistaking what she was insinuating, and the Duke did not criticise her fidgeting again. But he knew that it had begun to annoy him more and more.

The collection-plate was handed round and the Duke noticed that Lorena placed a shilling in it. The Vicar accepted the collection at the altar, then blessed the congregation.

Having knelt for a short time, he then proceeded once again to the Duke's pew, because His Grace always left the Church before the rest of the congregation.

For the first time the Duke leant towards Lorena and spoke to her.

"Will you come back with me?" he asked.

He knew that the manner in which she obeyed was part of her School training, and they walked down the aisle side-by-side behind the Vicar.

"Good-bye, Your Grace," the Cleric said at the door. "It has been an honour and a pleasure to have you with us."

"It was a very interesting sermon, Vicar," the Duke replied. "I must congratulate you."

Actually he had not listened to it, but the elderly man flushed with pleasure.

The carriage was waiting outside, a footman holding open the door.

Lorena looked up at the Duke.

"I walked here," she said.

"I hope you will drive back with me," he replied.

"May I? I would like that."

With a gesture of his hand he indicated that she should step into the carriage first, and as they drove away he said:

"I suppose I should have anticipated that you might wish to go to Church. How did you know about the Service?"

"I asked Emily, the maid who is looking after me," Lorena replied. "Do none of your other guests go with you to Church on Sunday?"

"I expect most of them attend Services in their own villages when they are at home, as I do," the Duke said evasively. "But as your father was a Parson, I suppose that as far as you are concerned it is a habit which you are not likely to break."

"I have never wanted to," Lorena replied. "When I am in Church I not only feel near to Papa, but also, as he always said, it gives me the power to face any difficulties and problems that might arise in the week ahead."

"Power?" the Duke questioned. "What do you mean by that?"

"Papa said we could draw on a life-force which is God Himself. It flows into us when we pray; then, if you want to help other people, they can draw on it because it is there inside one."

Lorena spoke quite simply and unaffectedly, and the Duke thought over what she had said before he remarked:

"I think that is an excellent explanation of what religion should do for people, but too often it fails lamentably."

"I know it is also what the Catholics believe," Lorena said, "and they draw their power not only from their Priests but from their holy images."

As if she felt that the Duke was waiting for an explanation, she went on:

"I have seen them so often in Rome kneeling in front of a statue of one of their Saints, or a holy painting, and I knew they were not only praying for help or for something they particularly desired, but they felt they were receiving some special power from the object to which they were praying."

"I understand what you are saying," the Duke said, "and it interests me enormously. On my travels I have often wondered what the Catholics who I have seen lighting candles and praying in their Churches were doing. Now you have explained it to me."

"I suppose," Lorena said, "that somebody as important as you, with so many people depending upon you, needs more power than someone as young and insignificant as myself."

"Are you suggesting that I should pray more fervently than anyone else?" the Duke asked in a slightly cynical voice.

"You do not need to pray as much as I must do," Lorena replied. "At the same time, there is nobody who does not need to link up with the force and the power of God. Even Christ had to do that."

The Duke thought that if the house-party could

overhear this conversation taking place between him and a girl of eighteen, they would not believe it.

He could not remember talking about God and prayer with anybody since he was a child.

At Oxford he and his friends had sometimes analysed their impulses and their actions, and discussed in a somewhat abstract manner the difference between various religions.

But now, listening to Lorena, he thought that she made the whole of living seem simple, and yet he knew how laughable his friends would find it.

It was so easy to mock her beliefs, to make a joke of the contention that a man like himself could draw his power from God.

He wondered if he should warn her to be careful with whom she discussed such things. Then he told himself that there was a purity and an innocent sincerity about her which any decent man would respect.

But he knew that this theory did not include women, especially a woman like Daisy.

It suddenly struck him that Daisy was not a good woman in any way. She was bad, and for the first time in many years he questioned his own interest in a woman who had few of the characteristics which he really admired.

They had almost reached the front door before Lorena said in a small voice:

"I am ... sorry if what I have said has ... bored you. Mama always said . . . one must never . . . thrust one's own opinions on . . . other people."

"You have not thrust on me anything that I was not extremely interested to hear," the Duke replied.

He knew by her smile that his answer pleased

her. Then the door of the carriage was opened and the drive was over.

*　　*　　*

Lorena spent a happy morning with Sir Hugo, looking round the stables.

He told her it was expected at Mere, as it was in most large houses, that on Sunday morning the guests should visit the stables.

The grooms had certainly gone to a great deal of trouble in preparing for them, Lorena noticed.

The passages had been freshly sanded, there was a straw plait to edge each stall, and the horses had been brushed and groomed until their coats shone like satin.

Lorena and Sir Hugo had not been at the stables for long before they were joined by Lord Carnforth, who was talking about his own horses, Perry Gillingham, and three other members of the house-party.

"You are up bright and early, Miss Benson," Lord Dartford said to Lorena.

She was going to reply that she had been up a long time because she had been to Church, but then she thought it might sound as if she were being critical of those who had not attended the Service, so she merely smiled and replied:

"It is too lovely a day to stay in bed."

"I agree with you, but we were all too late last night pursuing 'Lady Luck,' who certainly turned her back on me!"

"Did you lose a great deal of money?" Lorena asked sympathetically.

"More than I could afford," he replied.

She looked at him in a puzzled fashion and after a moment he said:

"I know you are thinking that I am a fool, and that is what I am thinking myself. Like all gamblers, I am always certain that the next card I turn up will win me a fortune."

"I read once," Lorena said, "that the odds against anyone who plays continually being an over-all winner at the card-tables are enormous!"

"You are telling me what I already know! As I have told you, I am a fool, but perhaps in such company I am too proud to say I cannot really afford to play for such high stakes."

"It is wrong that you should be expected to do so," Lorena said. "I think if I were the Duke I would . . ."

She had no chance to say more, for at that moment a voice behind her asked:

"Did I hear you say 'if I were the Duke'? I would be interested to hear the end of that sentence."

"If you had not interrupted, Alstone," Lord Dartford interposed before Lorena could reply, "you would have heard what Miss Benson had to say, and actually I think it would have been sheer common sense."

"I am listening," the Duke said.

"I would not like . . . you to think I was . . . criticising," Lorena said quickly. "It was . . . only an . . . idea."

The Duke's lips twisted.

"Another?" he said. "What is it this time?"

Lorena looked at Lord Dartford as if for permission to repeat what he had said.

"All right," he said with a smile, "tell the Duke if

you want to. It will not do any harm for him to
know the truth."

"The truth about what, Lionel?" the Duke enquired.

"Miss Benson will tell you that."

"What I was ... saying," Lorena said in a rather
small voice, "was that if I were ... Your Grace, I
would not ... allow people to ... lose in my home
more than they could really ... afford."

She saw the look of incredulity in the Duke's
eyes.

"Not because I think gambling is ... wrong,"
she continued, "although I do not understand why
it has such an attraction for some people ... it is
simply because I would want ... my guests to
be ... happy."

Both of the men to whom she was speaking were
listening, and she went on:

"No-one can be happy if he feels, as this gentleman does ... that he has been very ... foolish in
losing so much ... money in a game in which he
had really little ... chance of ... winning."

She stopped speaking and saw that the Duke
was astounded. Then he asked:

"Is this the truth, Lionel?"

"I am afraid it is."

"I realised that Arthur was making a killing last
night, but I hoped you had the sense to stop before
you were seriously involved."

"You must blame your good wines for giving me
a false optimism," Lord Dartford replied.

The Duke was frowning.

"I think Miss Benson is right. High stakes
should be kept for the Clubs and not permitted
in private houses, where it is difficult for guests to

break up a table or go to bed sooner than anyone else. I blame myself for letting this happen."

"No, no!" Lord Dartford said. "You must not do that. It is entirely my own fault. I made a fool of myself. I cannot imagine why I bothered Miss Benson with my troubles. Let us go and look at the horses."

As he spoke, he turned away abruptly and walked into the stables.

Lorena looked up at the Duke.

"I am . . . sorry for . . . him."

"I will put things right somehow," the Duke replied. "You are not to worry about it."

"I will try not to," Lorena said, "but . . ."

"I told you to leave everything to me," the Duke interrupted. "Let us also go and look at the horses."

He walked to the stables as he spoke and joined several others who were admiring the stallion he had ridden yesterday morning.

Lorena went to her uncle's side, and after a moment, when they had moved into another stall and were out of ear-shot of the others, he said:

"What were you talking to Lord Dartford about?"

"He is upset because he lost a great deal of money last night," Lorena explained.

"So did a number of others," Sir Hugo replied, "but they are too sporting to whine about it."

"He was not whining," Lorena retorted. "He was just admitting to me that he had been very foolish."

"I see you are always prepared to support the under-dog."

"But of course!" Lorena replied. "Those at the top do not need any help, least of all from me!"

Her uncle laughed, then the conversation turned

to horses and it was difficult to think of anything else.

It was nearly luncheon-time before they had walked back to the house, and Lorena, having tidied herself, came down to the Blue Drawing-Room, where she knew they were to congregate.

Most of the house-party were there and they all had glasses of champagne in their hands as she entered.

Her uncle was at the far end of the room, and she had started to walk towards him when the Countess of Hellingford detached herself from the people to whom she had been talking and turned to face her.

She was looking, Lorena thought, exceedingly beautiful in a very elaborate gown of chiffon and lace, with five ropes of pearls round her neck and diamond ear-rings which glittered with every movement she made.

Lorena looked at her and smiled in admiration. Then as she saw the expression in the Countess's eyes and realised that she was about to speak to her, she stopped still.

"I understand, Miss Benson," the Countess said in a voice that was clear enough to be heard by everybody in the room, and which also had a note of almost icy venom in it, "that you accompanied His Grace to Church this morning. Surely, ignorant though you may be, you are nevertheless aware that it is not correct for an unmarried girl to go driving alone with a man?"

It seemed to Lorena that everybody in the room was suddenly silent as the Countess's voice rang out as accusingly as if she were standing in the dock.

For a moment she was too surprised to reply, then she answered:

"I am sorry . . . I do not think of His Grace . . . as being a man."

It was the child-like, innocent way in which she spoke that prevented those who were listening from finding anything funny in what she had said.

Then, before the Countess could answer, Sir Hugo came to the rescue.

"If, Daisy, I had realised," he said, "how conscious *you* are of the proprieties, I would of course have accompanied Lorena to Church to see that she did not do anything so outrageous as to share a hymn-book with Alstone or wink at a Choir-boy!"

The mocking manner in which Sir Hugo spoke and the way he accentuated the words "you" and "proprieties" made everybody laugh, and there was no doubt that they were glad to relieve the tension by doing so.

But the Countess was not to be defeated.

"If you cannot look after your niece properly, Hugo," she said, "I am sure Kitty will be only too willing to oblige when she returns from her little trip to Suffolk, or was it actually Dorset which drew her?"

This, everybody knew, was a spiteful reference to Kitty's latest admirer, whose name was Lord Dorset.

Lorena did not understand, but everybody else in the room understood that Daisy was hitting back at Hugo not only for what he had said but for having a niece who had engaged the Duke's attention, if only for the time they had been in Church.

"How fortunate you are," Sir Hugo retorted,

"that, unlike Kitty, *your* journey need not take you any farther than Mere!"

Again there was laughter. A wordy duel between two members of the Windlemere Set was always amusing and far more entertaining than any drama that took place in the Theatre.

"Daisy will be out for Hugo's blood after this!" somebody remarked in a low voice.

"And for the girl's," was the reply.

Sir Hugo put his arm round Lorena's shoulders.

"I am not going to offer you a glass of champagne," he said, "as I think you would not care for it at this hour of the morning, but I am sure you would enjoy a non-alcoholic drink—apple-juice, for instance."

"That . . . would be . . . l-lovely."

Lorena stumbled a little over the words, knowing that although it was stupid of her, she felt shaken by the manner in which the Countess had spoken and by the animosity in her eyes.

'I wonder why she hates me,' she thought, and could find no explanation.

Only when she went in to luncheon and saw the Countess talking to the Duke did she understand.

Lorena thought she must have been blind not to realise it before, and she knew that she had told the truth when she had said she did not think of the Duke as a man.

Of course he was a man; in fact he was the most attractive, handsome man she could ever imagine. But she supposed that because he was so magnificent and so exactly what she had hoped for, she had thought of him as being like a King or a god in Ancient Greece—omnipotent, not human.

He had been so kind to her, letting her ride with

him, driving her back from Church, but all the time they had talked together it had never crossed her mind that she was with what her mother would have called "a young man."

She remembered hearing her mother say in the past:

"I know, darling, when you grow up there will be lots of young men to admire you and who will want to dance with you.

"I hope one day you will meet a young man with whom you will fall in love as I fell in love with your father."

'Mama was "in love" with Papa.'

Lorena thought the words beneath her breath, and she knew that what the Countess felt for the Duke was love. She was "in love" with him and was jealous because he had been to Church with somebody else.

It was ridiculous, of course, but Lorena knew from her books that jealousy caused people to behave violently, like Othello in Shakespeare's tragic play.

'It was . . . wrong of me to drive with him . . . alone,' she thought to herself.

She had suggested that she should walk home, but how could she explain that to the Countess?

Then she remembered that the Countess had a husband.

Her uncle had mentioned him, wondering how many lions he had shot in Africa.

He had not been talking to her but to several other people, and the Marchioness of Trumpington had said:

"There is one lioness he should have taken with him, or shot before he left!"

There was a burst of laughter at this, but Lorena had not understood. Now she thought the Marchioness must have been referring to the Countess of Hellingford.

'Perhaps I ought to explain to her,' Lorena thought, 'that I did not mean to go driving with the Duke and I do not think of him as a young man in the same way that she does.'

Then she asked herself if that was quite true.

Now that she thought about it, the Duke was very much a man, and no doubt that was really why she had enjoyed being with him; and it would be very, very disappointing if she could never be with him in the same way again.

It had been so exciting to ride alone with him, and it had been even more thrilling when they had breakfasted together and talked in the farm-house.

He seemed to understand what she was trying to say, and it suddenly struck her that of all the men in the party, even her uncle, the Duke was the one person who would not laugh at her "ideas," as he called them.

'I like him! I like him very much!' Lorena thought to herself.

It seemed unfair that the Countess should wish to keep him all to herself.

Lorena wondered whether if she was in love with a man, especially with one as handsome as the Duke, she would be jealous too, and rude to other women simply because he had talked to them.

"You are very silent," said Kelvin Fane.

Once again he was sitting next to her at a meal.

"What are you thinking about?"

Because Lorena felt that she knew him, without

considering what she should say, she told the truth.

"I was thinking about the Duke."

"I suggest you think about somebody else," he said, "unless you want Daisy to scratch your eyes out!"

Lorena was still for a moment, then she said:

"Is she . . . very much in . . . love with him?"

"She thinks she is."

"A-and . . . the Duke?"

"That is a question he should answer for himself. Anyway, it is much the best for you not to concern yourself with his affairs."

"Yes . . . of course."

Lorena felt humbly that it had been presumptuous of her to ask the questions which she had already asked.

"You are much too young to be at a party like this," Major Fane said sharply.

"I appreciate that everybody here is . . . older than . . . I," Lorena answered, "but I am trying not to be a . . . nuisance when Uncle Hugo has been so . . . kind as to . . . bring me."

"You are not in the least a nuisance," Major Fane replied. "The only trouble is that you are 'out of your depth' and you may get hurt in the process of trying to swim to safety."

"Why . . . should I be . . . hurt?"

She thought Major Fane was going to give her an explanation, but then he obviously changed his mind.

"I will tell you another time," he said, "but if you take my advice, you will leave the Duke alone."

He paused before he asked:

"Do you promise to do that?"

"I will . . . try," Lorena answered.

Even as she spoke, she knew that it was something which she did not wish to do.

She liked the Duke and wanted to be with him.

Chapter Five

After luncheon, as if he wanted to make up to her for the uncomfortable feeling caused by the Countess, Sir Hugo suggested to Lorena that they should go riding.

She enjoyed their ride, although she felt slightly guilty when her uncle spoke as if it were the first time that she had been on one of the Duke's horses.

Too late she felt that she should have told him what she had been doing yesterday morning when she got back to Mere.

But because she had already had breakfast in the farm-house and therefore did not need another one, she had not met her uncle until later in the morning.

As he was with a number of other people there seemed to be no point in drawing attention to herself by saying that she had been riding with the Duke.

"I should have remembered yesterday that you would like to ride," Sir Hugo said after they had galloped over the Park-land. "But make quite sure while you are here that you take every opportunity of enjoying the Duke's outstanding horses."

It was strange, Lorena thought, but she could not help feeling disappointed—or was it depressed?—at the thought that she would not be able to ride again alone with the Duke.

Looking back on her first ride early in the morning when the mist was on the lake and she and the Duke had galloped for a long time before they spoke to each other, it had been an enchantment which she could not put into words.

Then they had talked together in the farm-house and he had been so understanding, and she thought now that she should have realised at the time that it was too wonderful an experience to be repeated.

Sir Hugo interrupted her thoughts by saying as their horses moved side-by-side:

"Are you enjoying yourself, Lorena?"

"Very, very much, Uncle Hugo!"

"I am sorry that things were somewhat awkward this morning, but Daisy is a very difficult woman."

Lorena did not reply, and after a moment he went on:

"As of course you are well aware, it is quite wrong for any lady to make scenes in such a manner, and she certainly had no right to attack you for doing nothing more reprehensible than going to Church. But you will find, when you have lived in the world as long as I have, that one has to take these things as they come."

Lorena gave a little laugh.

"That is what my Nanny used to say when I was a child."

"It is quite a good motto for all of us," Sir Hugo

said, "and my Nanny used to say: 'Never expect too much, so you won't be disappointed'!"

Lorena laughed.

"I am sure mine said the same. She was full of wise sayings, and sometimes when I remember them now, they are helpful."

"I want to say," Sir Hugo said, as if he was following the train of his own thoughts, "that I am very proud of the way you have behaved. I am aware how difficult it must be for a girl to be pitchforked straight from School into a party at Mere, where everyone knows everybody else. But you have managed most successfully."

"Thank you, Uncle Hugo. It is very kind of you to say that."

"Sometime we must have a talk about your future," Sir Hugo went on, "but not until the end of the week, when we have to leave. I want you to enjoy yourself."

Lorena could not help a little tremor of fear and she was certain from the way he spoke that what he would tell her at the end of the week would not be good news.

'What will happen to me?' she wondered. 'Where will I go? Who shall I be with?'

It struck her almost despairingly that the one person she might never see again would be the Duke.

She had promised Major Fane that she would try to leave the Duke alone, but she could not help thinking of him, and later in the afternoon it was impossible to do anything else.

When she and her uncle got back to Mere he told her he was going to play Bridge and Lorena therefore went in search of Mr. Ashley.

Surprisingly, although it was Sunday she found that he was in his office.

"Perhaps I ought not to ask you today of all days," she said, "but could you show me some more of the house?"

"I should be delighted to do so, Miss Benson," he replied. "When His Grace is in residence, Sunday is the same as any other day to me."

He took Lorena round the Picture-Gallery, the Orangery, the Library, and a number of State Reception-Rooms in which Robert Adam had designed not only the walls and ceilings but also the glorious gold furniture, which made Lorena think once again that Mere was a fairy-tale Palace.

When they came to what Mr. Ashley told Lorena was called the Silver Sitting-Room, she saw there some more-modern paintings than in the other rooms, and these included a recent one of the Duke, very resplendent in the robes he had worn at the Coronation of King George V.

Lorena stood looking at it, feeling, because it was so well painted, almost as if she could talk to him as she had done this morning when they drove back from Church.

Then Mr. Ashley said:

"The sketch over the mantelpiece by John Sargent is of the Duchess on her wedding-day."

Lorena looked at him in astonishment.

"The Duchess?"

"The Duke was married. Did you not know that?"

"I had no idea."

"It was twelve years ago, when His Grace was just twenty-one, and the Duchess was killed in a fall out hunting before they had been married a year."

"How terrible!" Lorena exclaimed.

Then because she could not help herself, she asked:

"Was ... His Grace very ... upset?"

"It was a tragedy for everyone concerned," Mr. Ashley replied. "Now, let me show you these children's paintings by Hoppner, which are considered to be very fine examples of his work."

Lorena sensed that Mr. Ashley did not wish to speak any further about the Duchess. At the same time, she found it very hard to take in anything else the Curator was saying.

The Duke had been married!

She did not know why, but it was quite a shock.

It had never occurred to her that he had had a wife at Mere and that he was a widower.

Perhaps, she thought, he had been desperately unhappy at losing her and very lonely, and that was why he filled his life with friends who were witty and amusing and kept him entertained.

'I know so little about him,' she thought to herself.

Before they left the Silver Sitting-Room her eyes went back again to the Duke's portrait, thinking that the artist had captured his look of aloofness and also the impression he conveyed of being imperious and overwhelming.

It was difficult to gauge what the Duchess had been like, except that she was attractive with dark hair and large dark eyes.

'Perhaps he only likes dark-haired women,' Lorena thought.

Then she remembered that the Countess of Hellingford was certainly not dark but fair and very Junoesque.

"I am small and insignificant beside her, and also the Duchess," Lorena murmured to herself.

Then she remembered that she was breaking her promise to Major Fane.

"He will never know it," she excused herself, "nor will the Duke."

At the same time, when she was dressed for dinner she could not help hoping that she would not look too unattractive in comparison with the beautiful guests whom she had described to the Duke as looking like "swans gliding over a lake."

She was certain that they would, each of them, wear a gown that they had not worn before, their jewels would be spectacular, and the things they would say would amuse the Duke and the gentlemen whom they sat next to at dinner, as she was unable to do.

'Major Fane is right,' she thought as she looked in the mirror. 'I am too young, and it is only out of kindness to Uncle Hugo that anyone even speaks to me.'

Because she had only two evening-gowns, tonight she put on the one she had worn the night she had arrived.

It had seemed so attractive when she had chosen it in Rome.

Now she thought it was too plain and she wished that she could be covered with the frills of tulle and swirls of chiffon and especially the glittering jewels which made the other women shine like stars in the sky.

A knock on her door interrupted her thoughts, and when Emily went to open it Lorena thought despairingly that not even flowers could make her look anything but a School-girl.

Emily came to her side to say:

"Look, Miss. There's no choice tonight, as His Grace has sent these especially for you."

"Especially for me?" Lorena repeated.

Her heart gave a sudden jump because he had thought of her, because he had been kind enough to remember that she would have no diamonds or emeralds, no rubies or sapphires, to brighten her appearance.

Instead, on the tray there was a corsage of orchids and what appeared to be a wreath of them to wear on her head.

They were not in the least like the orchids she had worn on the first night. These were very pale pink and different from any flowers Lorena had ever seen before.

"They're very beautiful, Miss," Emily said. "They must be some of the rare species which His Grace grows in the Orchid-House. My father's one of the gardeners who looks after them, and he says His Grace has them sent from all sorts of outlandish places all over the world."

"These are certainly very beautiful!" Lorena exclaimed. "And there is a wreath for my hair!"

"Yes, Miss, and if you like, I'll pin it at the back of your head like one of them tiaras they wears in Russia."

Lorena knew what she meant, and asked with a smile:

"Have you seen them?"

"Yes, Miss. There was a Princess staying here last year and when she came to dinner, she wore a tiara that were an arch over the top of her head, and that's what these orchids can do for you."

Lorena thought they certainly made her look

quite different, and the pale pink of the flowers seemed to transform the severity of her gown, so that it made a perfect foil for them.

She pinned the corsage low down between her breasts, and when she looked at her reflection in the mirror she knew that her eyes were shining and she was no longer afraid of seeming small and insignificant.

He had thought of her! He had sent her the flowers, but she must never say so in case it made the Countess angry.

There was another knock at the door and Sir Hugo came into the room.

"You are ready, my dear?" he asked. "We must not be late."

"Yes, Uncle Hugo. I am ready."

"That is a very pretty wreath you have on your head..." he began; then he stopped, and exclaimed: "They are real! I thought when I came into the room that the flowers must be artificial."

"No, they are real," Lorena replied.

"They are certainly more attractive than any flowers I have seen for a long time," Sir Hugo said. "Well, come along or I shall be too late to have a drink before dinner."

They walked down the staircase, Lorena hoping that nobody else would think it strange that she was wearing such beautiful flowers.

She was not only afraid that if they did the Countess would be angry, but she thought somehow that even to discuss them might spoil the joy she felt because the Duke had taken the trouble to send them to her.

Fortunately, everybody in the Blue Drawing-Room was too engrossed in conversation to notice

her, except, although she might have been mistaken, she thought that the Duke glanced in her direction, then away again.

A hand touched hers and the Marchioness of
Trumpington drew her to one side.

"I am sorry, dear child," she said, "if you were
upset by Daisy's being so unkind before luncheon.
Had I known you wished to go to Church, I would
have gone with you."

"That would have been very kind of you,"
Lorena said, "but I did not want to be a trouble to
anybody."

"No, of course not, and that is the last thing you
are," the Marchioness said reassuringly. "Daisy is
absurdly jealous of anybody who even speaks to
the Duke, and being pretty, as you are, always has
its penalties."

"I certainly do not feel pretty when I look at
you," Lorena said in all sincerity.

The Marchioness was looking very beautiful in a
gown of Nile-blue tulle which accentuated the
red of her hair.

She wore a necklace and a small tiara of aqua-
marines, which had just become fashionable, and a
bracelet of the same stones on her wrist.

She smiled at the compliment, but before she
could reply, Lord Gilmour joined them, saying:

"Daisy is showing off like a peacock with two
tails! But as far as I am concerned, there is only
one beautiful woman in the room, and that is you,
Enid!"

There was a note in his voice which made
Lorena look at him in surprise. Then as she saw
the expression in his eyes, she drew in her breath.

Lord Gilmour was in love with the Marchioness

of Trumpington! At the same time, she was sure that they both were married.

She felt bewildered, and when they went in to dinner she looked up and down the table, wondering how many of the men present were in love with women who were not their wives.

She saw that once again the Countess of Hellingford was making every effort to capture the Duke's attention; and the Marchioness, with a very soft expression in her eyes, was listening to what Lord Gilmour was saying.

Opposite her, the Viscountess of Storr was having an obviously intimate and very personal quarrel with Major Fane.

She was pouting and shrugging her shoulders, and he was frowning, obviously put out by what she was saying.

Lorena's eyes rested for a moment on her uncle.

He, at least, did not seem to be engaged particularly with any of the ladies present.

Then she remembered the tone in which the Countess of Hellingford had said, when referring to her Aunt Kitty:

"Or was it actually *Dorset* which drew her?"

It was only after luncheon that Lorena understood that the Countess had been referring not to the County of that name but to a person.

She had not even been aware that there was someone called Lord Dorset until just before they were going riding, when she heard her uncle say to his valet:

"This is not my whip. Mine has a gold band round it."

The man looked at it.

"I'm sorry, Sir," he said apologetically. "I picked

it up in a hurry when we were packing to come
here, and I must have brought His Lordship's
instead of yours."

"Then see that it is returned to Lord Dorset as
soon as we return to London," Sir Hugo said
sharply. "And another time do not be so careless."

"I'm very sorry, Sir," the valet said again.

At the time, Lorena had thought that her uncle
seemed unnecessarily put out, until she realised
that the name rang a bell.

It was all very complicated, she thought; and
then, almost like the pieces of a puzzle falling into
place, she began to understand some of the things
that had worried her.

Aunt Kitty and Lord Dorset!

No wonder there was no place for her in her
uncle's house in Belgrave Square, or for that matter
at his home in the country.

She found herself remembering how her father
had talked of the Marriage-Service as a sacrament,
sacred and holy, and of course the vows the bride
and bridegroom took could never be broken.

Once her father had come home looking upset
and her mother had asked:

"What is the matter, darling? What is troubling
you?"

"It is the wedding at which I have just offici-
ated," her father replied. "I felt the whole atmos-
phere was wrong and there was not a genuine
prayer or act of faith in the whole Church."

"Perhaps you were mistaken."

Her father shook his head.

"No, I could feel it vividly. I knew the bride was
marrying the bridegroom for his money, and he
was content with the deal because his bride moves

in a higher social circle than the one into which he was born."

Lorena's mother had risen from the table to kiss her husband and say:

"You must not take these things to heart, dearest."

"I like the Marriage-Service to be one of dedication and a union of love," Lorena's father had said positively.

"Like ours," her mother had replied softly, "and that is how it will be when you marry young Wilcox tomorrow. I have never known two people more in love. I always thought she was rather a plain girl, but now she is almost a beauty!"

Lorena heard her father laugh and knew how cleverly her mother had spirited away his depression.

There had been many other occasions when he had believed that he had joined together two people who would find happiness because they were meant for each other.

Wealth, circumstance, and social position had no importance for him; it was only love that counted.

Looking back, Lorena realised that the people who felt like this were usually humble people; young men and women who lived in the village or others who were more well-to-do but did not aspire to any great social heights.

'Perhaps money corrupts,' she thought.

Then she told herself that if the person who possessed money had the right sort of character and high ideals, then no amount of it could really change or destroy them.

Then she rebuked herself for being selfish and thinking about herself instead of trying to entertain the gentlemen on either side of her at the dinner-table.

She turned to the man on her right and tried to find out what was his particular interest. She managed to have quite interesting conversations with both her partners before the elaborate, seven-course meal came to an end.

After dinner, in the Drawing-Room, Lorena was wise enough to go at once to the Marchioness of Trumpington's side, who smiled at her.

"I wonder," Lorena asked her, "if I could play the piano. If I played very softly it would not interrupt anything anyone was saying."

The Marchioness guessed that she was afraid of becoming involved with the Countess, and she said at once:

"It would be a very good idea, and I would like to hear you play. I am sure you had a good Teacher in Rome."

"An Italian to whom music was his whole life," Lorena replied.

As she spoke, she went to the piano which stood in an alcove.

It was a magnificent Broadway, and as Lorena sat down and her hands touched the keys, she knew that she might never again have the opportunity of playing on such a fine instrument.

But that, of course, was on a par with everything else at Mere.

She chose first the quiet music of Chopin. She was determined not to give the Countess an opportunity to find fault and say that she was interrupting anything which was being said.

Tonight Daisy Hellingford was looking not only beautiful but spectacular, and she was obviously holding court amongst the other ladies. She was queening it over them as if by right of the position, Lorena thought, which she assumed because she loved the Duke and he loved her.

It gave Lorena a strange pain to think of it, although why it should, she had no idea. It was the same feeling, she realised, that she had experienced when she learnt that the Duke had been married.

Then she told herself that it was just imagination, and began to concentrate almost fiercely on what she was playing.

From Chopin her fingers turned to the romantic music of Offenbach, and then as the gentlemen entered the Drawing-Room she felt there was no need for her to continue to play and she was now safe from the Countess.

As she saw the Duke walking down the room towards the ladies grouped at the far end of it, she rose from the piano and, moving swiftly, slipped out through the nearest French-window onto the terrace outside.

It was a very warm night without a breath of wind, the stars bejewelled the sky, and there was a moon throwing its light over the garden, making the lake look silver and magical.

Without planning where she would go, Lorena moved along the terrace in her satin slippers, descended some steps onto the lawn, and walked away from the house.

It seemed ridiculous, now that she was free of it, that she should have been afraid of anyone, but she knew she did not want the Countess of Hellingford to spoil the enchantment she had felt ever since she had come to Mere.

Already it was as if part of the dream had been

torn aside and she was seeing and hearing things she had not noticed before, and what she had learnt was detracting from the beauty which had held her spellbound.

'It is like waking up,' Lorena thought, 'when I want to go on dreaming.'

She felt as if the fairy-story was slipping away from her and all she would be left with was a reality which might be ugly and unpleasant.

The loveliness of the garden was like a cool hand on a fevered brow.

Whatever was happening in the brilliantly lit Drawing-Room she had left behind her, here was peace, the quiet and the wonder of the night.

There was the fragrance of the night-scented stock, the shrill squeak of an occasional bat overhead, and there was the moon, the stars, and the feeling that she was surrounded by beings from another world, although she could not see them.

'Perhaps,' Lorena thought, 'they are the people who have lived at Mere, who once walked in the garden as I am doing to escape from their troubles and difficulties.'

Perhaps too, she thought, there were also celestial beings round her, who could move amongst mortals and influence them to seek for something higher than themselves, something that was definitely there but just out of reach.

By the time Lorena reached the water-lily pool, which was surrounded by a yew-hedge on which there were strange and skilfully cut examples of topiary work, she was lost in her imagination, happy in a manner which was impossible to describe.

With each step everything disturbing fell away

and she became spellbound because her whole being was uplifted spiritually.

In the centre of the water-lily pond was a carved
statue of Eros, holding in his arms a large fish from
whose mouth poured a stream of water into the
pool beneath him.

The moonlight made him silvery and very entic-
ing, and there was only the soft fall of the water
and the stars reflected on it.

Lorena looked up and felt as though something
within her, perhaps her heart, flowed up to the sky
and gave her the power of which she had spoken to
the Duke, the power that she knew came from God
and was His.

Then she heard footsteps coming towards her
along the path which had brought her to the
water-lily pool.

For a moment she drew in her breath, hoping,
with a hope which she could not repress, that it was
the Duke who had come to join her.

But instead in the moonlight she saw Major
Fane.

* * *

The Duke had been well aware when he
reached the end of the Drawing-Room that Lorena
had disappeared through the French-windows out
onto the terrace.

He could understand that she wanted to get
away, and when he had come into the Drawing-
Room he had actually been relieved to find that she
was nowhere near Daisy.

He wondered who had suggested to her that she
might play the piano and thought perhaps it was

Enid Trumpington. But he knew it would be unwise for him to ask questions.

"Are you going to gamble, Alstone?" Daisy
asked.

She was good-tempered tonight and the Duke
was not certain whether it was because she thought
she had won a battle or because he, to save Lorena
from her sharp tongue, had gone out of his way to
be pleasant to her.

"Of course," he replied. "I thought that was what
you would want."

"I won a little money last night," Daisy said,
"but not enough. You must sit near me, Alstone,
and bring me luck."

"I must see what my other guests wish to do
first," he said. "You go to the big table and get it
organised, you always do that so well."

Daisy smiled.

She was always delighted when the Duke treated
her as if she were the hostess at Mere, which was
definitely what she wanted to be.

'He is mine,' she thought to herself, 'and the
sooner everybody realises that I can prevent them
from being invited here if I wish, the better!'

It was a pretence that she knew had no substance
in fact, but Daisy could always believe what she
wanted to believe.

As she settled everybody into their places at the
Baccarat-table she did so in a manner which made
it quite obvious that she was running the show her
way and was the only one who counted.

Three of the guests wanted to play Bridge, and the
Duke had just found them a fourth player when
he noticed that Kelvin Fane was not at the

Baccarat-table as he had expected, but was walking through the open window onto the terrace.

The Duke was instantly aware that he was following Lorena, and he thought with a sudden irritation that it was too bad of Fane, after Daisy's behaviour before luncheon, to put the girl in danger of evoking a scene with Sarah Storr.

"This is the last time I shall ever invite a young, unmarried girl to one of my parties," he vowed to himself.

Then it struck him that it was not because Lorena was young and unmarried that she was causing trouble amongst his guests, but because she had an attraction that was unusual.

Whatever it might be, he was responsible for the girl, and Fane had no right to be alone with her in the garden, which would certainly infuriate Sarah and cause a great deal of comment, even if it was good-natured, from everyone else.

Therefore, at a moment when Daisy was busily engaged in dealing the cards, he went out onto the terrace and wondered in which direction Lorena had gone.

He was sure, although he did not know why, that she would find her way to the water-lily pool in the garden.

It was one of the loveliest of the small gardens that had been laid out by his grandmother, and even as a small boy he had found it particularly attractive.

There was also a herb-garden surrounded by red brick Elizabethan walls, there was a rose-garden that had a sun-dial in the centre of it, and there was a Japanese garden where all the trees and

shrubs were tiny dwarves of their much larger
species.

There were other gardens farther away from the
house, but the nearest was the water-lily garden,
and the Duke thought it one of the most beautiful.

He moved quickly over the soft lawn, and then
as he neared the garden he knew he had been right
in his assumption, for he heard voices.

His first impulse was to join Lorena and Kelvin
Fane. Then as he reached the yew-hedge he was
aware that he could hear what they were saying.

"It is very lovely here," Lorena said, "but I think
we ought to go back to the house."

"There is no hurry," Kelvin Fane replied. "Everybody is playing Bridge or Baccarat, and I want to
talk to you."

"What . . . about?"

"Yourself."

"I can only think how lovely the water-lily garden is."

"You are lovely too!"

"I think we . . . should go . . . back."

There was no doubt that Lorena was nervous,
and the Duke reached out his hands to part the
branches of the yew-hedge in front of him.

Through the space he made he could see her
quite clearly, standing by the little pool with the
moonlight lighting her face, while Kelvin Fane had
his back to him.

"I will take you back," Kelvin said, "but first,
because like you I find everything here so beautiful, I want to kiss you. You have never been kissed,
Lorena, and I want to be the first."

"No!"

Lorena had not moved, but she spoke positively.

"No?" Kelvin Fane questioned. "Why should you say that?"

"Because when I am . . . kissed, I think . . . perhaps it might be very . . . wonderful . . . but I would like the . . . man I kissed to be the man I would . . . marry."

There was a silence and the Duke knew that Kelvin Fane was surprised.

"I think," he said after a moment, "that you might find it difficult to know if you wish to marry a man unless you have kissed him first."

Lorena shook her head before she said:

"You may think it foolish of me . . . but I am sure that if I loved someone enough to want to . . . marry him . . . I would know it in my heart."

"Perhaps you are right," Kelvin Fane said, "but I still want to kiss you, Lorena. I want it more than I have wanted anything for a long time."

The Duke had the feeling that he was going to insist, and he thought angrily that this was something he could not allow.

He was ready to walk down the steps into the garden and interrupt Fane before he had time to frighten Lorena, but before he could do so, he heard her say:

"I think that if the lady who . . . loves you heard you say such things to me, she would be angry, and I would not blame her, because it is surely disloyal to love one woman and want to kiss another."

If Lorena had surprised Fane before, she had certainly succeeded in astonishing him now, the Duke thought.

"I am a free man," Fane said, as if he must excuse himself. "I belong to nobody, Lorena, and no-one can stop me from wanting to kiss you, nor is it disloyal."

"Then if it is not disloyal," Lorena replied, "it is unkind. I do not want to be unkind to anyone . . . and please . . . I do not want to be kissed."

There was something in the way she spoke, the little tremor in her voice, and the fact that in the moonlight she looked so lovely and yet so young.

She might in fact have been no older than the boy Eros standing in the centre of the water-lily pond; and as if she had used a weapon far more effective than the arrows Eros carried on his shoulder, Kelvin Fane capitulated.

"I will not do anything you would not wish me to, Lorena," he said, "but will you promise me something?"

"Another promise?" Lorena enquired.

"The promise I extracted from you at luncheon," he said, "was to save you from getting hurt by becoming involved with our host. What I am going to ask you now is something quite different."

"What is it?"

She was still a little nervous, still afraid, the Duke thought apprehensively, because she was now aware, as she might not have been before, that Kelvin Fane was a man and he desired something else.

"What I am going to ask you is that when we leave Mere I can see you. It is, as you have probably noticed, a little difficult here, and elsewhere it would be very different. I want to see you, Lorena, more than I can tell you."

"I would like to see you again," Lorena answered, "but I do not know where I shall be, where I am to live."

"That is immaterial," Kelvin Fane said. "I will find you. Then, Lorena, we can really get to know each other as I would like to do."

There was a note of urgency in his voice that made Lorena say again:

"I think we should go back."

She could not proceed down the path unless he stepped out of her way.

She took a hesitating step forward, then for a moment their eyes met, and the Duke, watching, was still, aware that it was a battle of wills.

It was strange, he thought, that anyone so young and so inexperienced as Lorena could fight one of the most experienced and certainly the most ardent lover in the Social World.

And yet, as he waited, almost holding his breath to see the result, Lorena won. Kelvin Fane stepped to one side and she passed him, then he walked after her down the narrow path which led out of the garden.

With a swiftness which was thanks to his athletic ability, the Duke moved away from the yew-hedge and by the time Lorena and Kelvin Fane emerged onto the lawn he was advancing towards them as if he were just coming from the house.

"There you are!" he exclaimed. "I came to tell you, Kelvin, that you are wanted at the Baccarat-table, or I think they want your money!"

"Then they are not going to have it!" Kelvin Fane replied. "I have no intention of playing to-night, and to tell the truth I am rather bored with Baccarat. I will cut in at Bridge, or, if you prefer, play you a game of Piquet."

There had been a momentary start at seeing the

Duke so near to them, but Kelvin Fane had spoken quite naturally.

Lorena had felt her heart leap with an irrepressible gladness as she saw the Duke coming towards them.

She had been afraid that Major Fane would insist on kissing her and she thought it would be undignified and embarrassing to have to struggle against him.

She had never before been in such a position with a man, and she had known when the Major said he wished to kiss her that she did not want him to, and the words in which she had refused him had come to her mind almost as if they were an inspiration from outside herself.

Still she had been afraid, but now that she saw the Duke, so tall, so broad-shouldered, she had an impulse to run towards him and tell him how frightened she had been and how glad she was that he was there.

Then as he joined them and they all three walked across the lawn back towards the lights gleaming golden from the windows onto the terrace, she knew that everything was wonderful again and her dream was still with her because the Duke was there too.

When they reached the terrace, the Duke deliberately stopped as they reached the light from the window to lean over the balustrade and look towards the lake.

"You had better go in, Kelvin," he said. "I will join you in a moment or two."

He knew as he spoke that Fane was an intelligent man and realised that for him to appear with

Lorena would give both Sarah and Daisy something to be unpleasant about.

Accordingly, Kelvin Fane walked in through the Drawing-Room window and Lorena heard the Marchioness call his name from the Baccarat-table.

"I think Mere is more beautiful by moonlight than at any other time," the Duke said conversationally to Lorena.

"I ... I suppose it was ... wrong of me to go alone into the garden," Lorena replied.

"Not wrong, perhaps unwise," the Duke answered.

"I am ... sorry ... I keep making mistakes."

"They are not really mistakes," the Duke said. "I do not want you to worry about them. What I want you to do is to go in now and play the piano very softly as you were doing when we joined you after dinner."

"I would like to do that. You do not think I shall be interrupting anybody?"

"You will not interrupt those who are gaming, and as they will know where you are, there will be no reason to gossip about you."

"I understand ... and it is very wise of you ... and once again I am ... sorry I was so ... foolish."

"When you have played enough," the Duke said, "you can either join us in the Ante-Room or, if you prefer, you can go to bed."

"That would not be rude?"

"No-one will think it rude that you are not throwing your money away on what you say is an odds-on chance that you will not win."

Lorena gave a little laugh.

"I would not gamble anyway, even if I had any

money. I will go to bed and read. I found some very exciting books in your Library this afternoon."

"I thought you would discover them sooner or later."

"I discovered other things as well, and Mr. Ashley says there are still more things for me to discover tomorrow."

"And when you have been everywhere, will you then be bored?" the Duke asked.

"Never! I could never be bored here!" Lorena said. "I believe that one is never bored with beautiful things, only perhaps sometimes with people."

He found some of the strange, perceptive things she said so unexpected, and she gave him a smile as she said:

"Good-night, Your Grace, and thank you again so very, very much for . . . everything!"

She slipped away from him as she spoke and went through the open window into the now-deserted Drawing-Room.

The Duke waited and after a moment there was a melody, played skilfully, he realised, by someone who loved music and had been well taught.

He listened to what she was playing and knew that it was in fact a little paean of gratitude for what she had seen and found at Mere.

She translated quite easily into music what she was saying and thinking.

He listened for some minutes, then sauntered slowly into the Ante-Room.

Daisy saw him and called out:

"Alstone, where have you been? There is a place here for you."

The Duke walked across to the table and sat down in the chair next to hers.

"Where have you been?" she asked again.

"Getting some fresh air," he answered. "I find it rather hot tonight."

He knew that by this explanation he allayed any suspicion she might be feeling.

"You should have let me know," she said automatically.

Then as she dealt him the cards, she said, almost under her breath so that only he could hear:

"Darling, I missed you! You know I hate you to be away from me even for a few minutes."

The way she spoke made the Duke feel that she was reaching out her hands and holding on to him, holding him captive, striving to make him her prisoner.

He felt an unusual anger rising within him.

He had no wish to be tied, no wish to belong to any woman, whoever she might be.

Then he remembered overhearing Kelvin Fane saying that he was free, and he knew it was a lie.

They were none of them free.

These women were determined to hold them enthralled, and the Duke was embroiled with Daisy as Lorena had known Kelvin was with Sarah.

"Dammit all!" he said to himself. "Am I man or a mouse that I should let this happen to me?"

He looked at his cards, then flung them down on the table.

"I have no wish to play tonight," he said. "It is too hot."

He pushed back his chair and rose to his feet as Daisy gave a cry of protest.

"But, Alstone! This is . . ."

The Duke knew what she was saying, but he would not listen to it.

He walked across the room to where Kelvin Fane was standing with an obstinate look on his face, listening to Sarah Storr, who had risen from the table to speak to him.

"I do not know about you, Fane," the Duke said, "but I would like a game of Billiards. Are you prepared to give me one?"

"Yes, of course!" the Major replied. "That is what I call a sensible suggestion."

"I want you to play Bridge with me," Sarah Storr protested.

"You have your four," Kelvin Fane replied.

The Duke had moved towards the door and the Major was following when Sarah Storr caught hold of his arm.

"Do not be too late," she said in a whisper. "I will be waiting for you, dearest."

Kelvin Fane did not reply.

He knew as he walked towards the Billiards-Room beside the Duke that he would not see Sarah again that night.

Chapter Six

The Duke was fast asleep when he was aroused by the growling of his dog Rufus, who always slept with him.

It was unusual for Rufus to wake him during the night, and as the Duke opened his eyes he thought it must be morning.

Then he saw that the room was completely dark except that he had pulled back the curtains before he went to bed because it was so hot, and he could see the stars in the sky.

Rufus growled again and the Duke wondered what could be upsetting him.

Then the dog went to the door, sniffing.

Now the Duke was sure that somebody was outside in the passage, and he wondered who it could be.

It was most unlikely that anyone was passing his room, because he was in the Master Suite, which, while on the first floor of the main building, was not near any of the other rooms except for one.

In that room slept the Countess, but it was most improbable that she should be moving about at this time of the night or coming to him.

He had not, in fact, as she had wished him to

do, gone to her room last night when they had come up to bed.

He knew that she was waiting for him to do so, as she had waited the night before, but he had no inclination to go to her and she was experienced enough in the handling of men not to press him.

Nevertheless, when they had all gone up the stairs together after the Baccarat was finished and the Duke's guests one by one had said good-night and gone to their own rooms, only Daisy had been left.

He had stopped outside her door.

"Good-night, Daisy," he said. "I am glad you won tonight."

"Must it be good-night?" she enquired.

She looked very beautiful in the light from the gold sconces in the corridor and the Duke could not understand his feeling that he had no wish to touch her.

He was even reluctant to raise her hand to his lips, though he felt obliged to do so.

"I am tired," he said.

As he spoke, he was ashamed of himself for giving such a banal reason, which he was sure Daisy would know was untrue.

He kissed her hand, and as, bewildered, she drew him a little towards her, he turned away.

"Good-night, Daisy," he said. "It is very late, so I am sure you will sleep well."

He knew she made a movement as if she would stop him, but he was moving away down the corridor to his own room and he did not look back.

Now as Rufus went on sniffing at the door, the Duke listened and waited tensely.

He thought it would be undignified and ex-

tremely embarrassing to have a scene with Daisy
at this moment, but his door did not open. Now he
felt certain, although he was not sure why, that
whoever it was had passed on down the corridor.

It suddenly struck him that there might be a bur-
glar in the house.

There were always night-watchmen on duty, but
he had thought for some time that they were getting old and he was thinking about installing one
of the new burglar-alarms which he had been told
were extremely effective.

It had never seemed necessary to guard against
burglars at Mere, but there had been talk lately of
robbers breaking into various large houses, and the
Duke knew that the treasures he possessed could
prove a great temptation to those who were known
as "collectors" and who often employed very dubi-
ous methods to add to their collections.

At last he sprang out of bed and, putting on his
slippers and a long velvet robe that was laid on a
chair, walked to the door.

Rufus was now growling as if he was still aware
of an intruder but it was already becoming a memory, something of the past.

Feeling his way, as he did not wish to put on the
light, the Duke found the handle of the door and
turned it softly.

Outside in the passage, as was usual when everybody had retired to bed, the night-footmen had
left only a few lights burning in each corridor.

The Duke advanced from his own room and
thought, although he could not be certain, that in
the shadows something moved at the far end of it.

Curious now, and determined to investigate, he
walked quickly towards the place where he thought

he had seen a movement, and only as he reached it did he notice at the end of the corridor the small twisting staircase which led up to the roof.

It had been so long since he had gone any farther along the corridor than to his own room that he had almost forgotten the staircase existed.

Now he was certain that whoever had disturbed Rufus had gone up the staircase as if to hide.

It flashed through his mind that burglars would find the huge roofs of Mere a convenient place not only to hide but to descend to the ground at a different point from where they had come in, thus escaping observation.

As he moved swiftly up the staircase he thought perhaps he had been rather foolish in not bringing a weapon of some sort with him.

There was always a revolver in one of the drawers in his bedroom, but a stout walking-stick or a poker would be just as effective if used by someone as strong and athletic as himself.

Then he thought with a smile that he could fight any ordinary intruder with his fists and enjoy doing so.

When he was at Oxford he had been the University's champion pugilist at his weight, and he had given a good account of himself in the ring when he was in the Army.

It struck him that he had not fought for some time and he might even enjoy a fight, as long as there were not too many men with whom to cope at the same time.

He reasoned that if there had been several, Rufus would have barked rather than just sniffed at the door and growled.

He reached the top of the staircase and in front

of him was the door which opened onto the roof,
and he saw that it was open.

He went out rather cautiously, then he saw
standing just ahead of him, looking towards the
East, a slim figure in white.

He knew at once who it was, and a perception
he had had before about Lorena told him why she
was there.

It was many years since the Duke had stood on
the roof to see the dawn break and he knew now
it was an experience that Lorena would want to
enjoy while she was at Mere.

Someone, and he suspected it must have been
Mr. Ashley, had told her how beautiful it could be.

Even as the Duke stood looking at her, he knew
that the sky was lightening and the brilliance of the
stars had begun to fade.

Now he could see Lorena's features, her small,
straight nose and pointed chin, silhouetted against
the sky.

Her head was lifted so that the long line of her
neck also was revealed, and she looked, he
thought, as if she were a statue put there like the
marble urns that surmounted the entrance of the
house.

He moved forward to stand beside her.

She did not turn her head but he knew she was
aware of him, and because he knew she would expect it of him, he stood looking towards the East
as she was doing without speaking.

The sky lightened further, and the first paleness
on the horizon deepened to gold, its rays moving
up to sweep away the sable of the night and the
stars which only in the West lingered now behind
them.

Then just before the sun itself appeared on the horizon, the Duke felt Lorena's hand slip into his.

He tightened his fingers on hers and knew as he did so that she gave a little quiver, although whether it was excitement because of what she was watching or because he was touching her, he did not know.

Then almost dramatically the sun was there, golden and radiant, at first a vivid streak of flame, then dazzling the eyes with the intensity of its fire.

The Duke knew that Lorena held her breath, at the same time holding tightly on to him, so that he felt they were joined in watching something so splendid, so overwhelmingly beautiful.

The glory in the East intensified, and it was day.

Still neither Lorena nor the Duke moved. Then he felt her hold on his fingers slacken, and because he knew she was spellbound he let her go.

She gave a deep sigh that seemed to come from the depths of her being.

She turned to look at him, her eyes holding the sunshine, and her face, he thought, was transfigured with a beauty he had never seen before.

She smiled at him, and then without speaking moved away across the roof and disappeared down the staircase up which she had come.

The Duke stood staring after her as if he could hardly believe that she had in fact left him.

It seemed somehow incredible that they should have gone through such a strange experience together and yet she had nothing to say about it.

But he knew that in leaving him she had done the right thing.

There were no words to describe what they had

seen, and to talk about it would somehow have spoilt what was too perfect to put into words.

He knew without being told that that was what Lorena had felt, and although it had surprised him, she had been right in behaving as she had. But it was, he thought, exactly what he might have expected of her.

The Duke looked away towards the sun.

It was shining now on the vast acres of his Estate and he could see the woods, the meadows, the streams, and the farms with their animals spread out before him, almost as if it were a map which could move and live.

'Mine, all mine,' he thought.

Then he knew it was much more than that.

It was a sacred trust that had been handed to him by his father and his ancestors before him, and one that he in his turn must hand to his son and those who would follow in his footsteps.

* * *

Lorena slept rather later than usual and when she awoke she felt as if she had experienced something so precious, so perfect, that she would hold it forever in her heart.

She knew that what made it more wonderful, more marvellous than it would otherwise have been, was the fact that the Duke had shared that magical moment with her.

She did not know how he was aware that she was on the roof. She only accepted like a small miracle that he should suddenly be beside her and without even thinking about it she could hold on to him.

When Mr. Ashley had mentioned that the view

from the roof was stupendous and the finest in the whole County, she had known the moment when she wanted to see it.

Often in Rome she had risen early to go to the window and watch the dawn break over the city, shining as if it were an act of faith, particularly on the Dome of St. Peter's.

She knew the view from the Convent would be nothing compared with the view that would be afforded at Mere, which was built on high ground and, being so tall, commanded over a great distance.

She had not been disappointed in what she had expected.

She had known it was a moment she would never forget, nor could she forget the feelings the Duke had evoked when his fingers had tightened on hers.

She was aware too, when she got back to her bedroom and slipped into bed, that what she felt was love. It was in fact what she had been feeling for him for a long time, but she had been afraid to give it a name even to herself.

"I love him!" she whispered. "And it is exactly what I expected love would be like, spiritual and perfect and like the sun, from God.

She wanted to pray in gratitude for the wonder she was feeling, but it was really a paean of joy because the emotions which rippled through her could not be expressed in any other way.

"I love him! I love him!" she said over and over again.

For the moment it did not dim her joy to know that he would never love her, that he would never be anything personal or intimate or other than what he had been when she first saw him, a Prince in a Fairy-Palace.

'Wherever I go, whatever happens to me,' she thought, 'he will always be there in my mind and nothing can ever take away from me the rapture I felt just now when we watched the dawn together.'

Vaguely, far away as if in the shadows, her brain told her that he belonged to the Countess, but for the moment even that was of no importance beside what she had felt and what in a way she had received, a blessing that could come only from God.

"To love anyone so wonderful is a privilege and an honour!" Lorena told herself. "And I can pray for him and feel that perhaps in a very small way my prayers will protect him."

She could not help feeling that the Countess was the wrong person for anybody so understanding and sympathetic as the Duke.

Then she told herself humbly that she was no judge and she understood that the Countess would fight to keep him. To lose such a man, if he had loved her, would be almost a death-blow.

Lorena fell asleep thinking of the Duke, and she was sure that while she slept she dreamt of him, and when she awoke much later it was to feel that in some way he was still with her and her hand was still held in his.

When she went downstairs, having already had breakfast, which Emily had brought to her room as she had slept so late, she found Sir Hugo and Perry waiting to take her riding.

She longed to ask where the Duke was, but while she was still wondering how to frame the question, Sir Hugo said:

"Most of the party have gone on without us, and the Duke is seeing his Agent, so we will not wait for him."

Lorena longed to reply that it was the one thing she wanted to do, but she knew her uncle would think it strange.

Instead, she mounted the horse that was waiting outside the door and tried to feel that she was so lucky to be riding that it would be shameful to ask for more.

She wanted the Duke to be there, wanted to see him riding his magnificent black stallion as if he were part of the horse, wanted to see his face, hear his voice.

They rode for nearly two hours, and then as they turned for home Lorena felt an inward excitement because in a very short while she would see the Duke again.

"I love him!" she said to herself. "But I must be careful. I must never let him guess for one moment what I feel, and most of all, I must never let anyone else have the slightest suspicion."

She knew the one person she feared if she became suspicious was the Countess.

As she thought of how beautiful Daisy Hellingford was, she felt as if a shadow passed across the sun.

* * *

The Duke was in his Library, signing some papers which his secretary had brought him, when the Countess came into the room.

She was looking extremely beautiful in a gown of pale mauve chiffon and a large-brimmed hat trimmed with wistaria.

"I am afraid I am busy, Daisy," the Duke said automatically, but his secretary said quickly:

"This is the last one, Your Grace. I must apologise for taking up so much of your time."

There was nothing the Duke could do in the circumstances, and as the secretary left the room with the signed letters, the Duke rose to his feet to walk to the fireplace where Daisy Hellingford was waiting for him.

"I did not expect you down so early, Daisy," he said. "In fact I intend to go riding now that I have finished my letters. Why do you not come with me?"

The Duke knew as he spoke that it was a quite pointless invitation because Daisy disliked riding and never got on a horse if she could help it.

"I want to talk to you, Alstone."

The Duke resigned himself to what he knew he would have to hear sooner or later.

"Do you want to talk here," he asked, "or shall we go out into the garden?"

"What I have to say should be said at once," Daisy replied, "and where it is said does not matter one way or the other."

"Very well," the Duke agreed.

"You are behaving in a very extraordinary manner, Alstone, and I want an explanation. First, ever since I arrived here there has been something going on between you and your friends about which I have not been informed; secondly, you have been avoiding me."

The Duke opened his lips to reply, but before he could speak she held up her hand.

"I have not finished," she said. "Last week in London you were somewhat evasive. I told myself that it was because we had too many parties to attend, too many people to see, but that here at Mere it would be different."

She paused for breath and the Duke began:

"Now listen, Daisy . . ."

"You listen to me!" she flashed. "I love you, Alstone! And I believed that you loved me, but you have not been near me since I arrived here. I want to know the reason why."

It was, the Duke knew, the crux of the whole problem.

He had told himself already that he had to accept it sooner or later, and as Daisy was intent on a show-down, there was nothing he could do but have it now.

He walked away from the hearth-rug towards the window, wondering, as he did so, why women must always give voice to what is quite obvious without the need of words.

He stood looking out at the sunshine, then said:

"I think, Daisy, we are both adult enough to accept things which happen to us in our lives without recriminations, without having to spell them out in words of two syllables."

There was no reply from Daisy for a moment, and he turned curiously to see an expression on her face which he supposed he might have anticipated.

It was one of astonishment.

"Are you saying that you are tired of me?" she asked after a moment in a strangled voice.

Even as she spoke there was a note in her voice which told the Duke that to her, such a development was completely and utterly inconceivable.

"I am not exactly tired," the Duke said evasively, "but I think, Daisy, we are both aware that our *affaire de coeur* has not quite the spontaneity and perhaps the excitement it had when it first started."

"That is a lie as far as I am concerned!" Daisy snapped. "I love you, Alstone, and *my* feelings have not changed."

"I do not think that is quite true," the Duke said. "At the same time, I am not prepared to argue about it. When we return to London I will send you a present which I hope you will always keep as a memento of the great happiness we have enjoyed with each other, and I hope we shall always remain friends."

As he spoke, he thought that it sounded priggish, but he could not imagine how else he could finish with Daisy. Certainly as far as he was concerned everything was over, and she had to accept it whether she wished to or not.

"Are you really brushing me off in this manner?" Daisy asked. "I have never been so insulted, never in the whole of my life! I can assure you, Alstone, you are making a very grave mistake, and it is something you will deeply regret."

There was no doubt that she intended to make him regret it, but for the moment the Duke could only bow before the storm, and there was no chance for him to say anything.

He had always been told that Daisy Hellingford had a temper, but while she was happy exerting her power over him and because he in many ways had found her fascinating, he had never seen her in a rage until now.

As he watched her working herself up into a flaming passion and heard the vitriolic reproaches

which dropped from her lips, he knew that the one
thing he really disliked was a woman who lost control of herself.

He supposed it might have been expected from
anyone like Daisy; if she was fiery in one way, she
would be fiery in another.

He felt, however, that she not only degraded
herself in losing her temper but also degraded him.

He wanted to stop her and prevent the scene between them from becoming uglier as it was doing
minute by minute, but it would have been easier
to halt a cyclone or calm a tempest at sea.

Daisy raged on and on, and the Duke found
himself disliking her more with every second that
passed.

*   *   *

Lorena walked in through the front door, followed by Sir Hugo and Perry.

"We have plenty of time to change before luncheon," Sir Hugo said as he glanced at the huge crys-
tal and gilt French clock which stood in a corner
of the Hall.

"Thank goodness for that!" Perry remarked before Lorena could answer. "I want to have a bath.
I have never known it to be as hot as it is today."

"It must certainly be nearly in the eighties," Sir
Hugo said.

As all three moved towards the staircase, Lord
Carnforth came from a Salon and walked towards
them.

"Have you had a good ride?" he asked.

"Delightful!" Sir Hugo replied. "I thought you
were going to join us."

"I was waiting for Alstone," Lord Carnforth said, "but I waited in vain."

He dropped his voice so that the servants would not hear, and added:

"Daisy is making a scene in the Library, and I should think the temperature at luncheon will be well below zero!"

"What has upset her?" Perry asked quickly.

"I have no idea," Lord Carnforth replied. "I only know that I have missed my ride!"

Lorena went up the stairs in silence.

She wondered what the Countess could be making a scene about now, and she hoped, with a little tremor of fear, that she had not in some mysterious way found out that she and the Duke had been on the roof together at dawn.

She felt sure it was impossible, and yet one never knew.

She wished, because she was frightened, that she did not have to go down to luncheon, but even if she did not do so, she would have to meet the Countess sooner or later, and if she was angry she was sure no-one could prevent her from saying so.

She wondered if she could confide in her uncle and tell him that although she had not meant to be alone with the Duke again, it had just happened because he had joined her.

Then she knew she could not bear to speak of that moment of happiness to anyone. It would spoil it.

It would spoil a perfect moment that she had placed in a shrine within herself so that it could be kept sacred from the world. Especially the world which contained the Duke's friends.

"Please . . . God . . . please do not let her . . . find out . . . where we were," she prayed.

She went on saying the same prayer all the time she was changing her clothes.

She went down to luncheon apprehensively, to find that most of the house-party who had gathered in the Blue Drawing-Room had their heads together and were talking in low voices, which meant that they were discussing their host and the Countess.

The Marchioness of Trumpington put out her hand to Lorena as she walked in, and drew her away from the others to move near a window.

"Come and talk to me, Lorena," she said. "I want you to tell me about your life at home when your father and mother were alive."

"I would like to do that," Lorena said simply, "but I am afraid you might find it rather dull. We lived in a small Vicarage in a very quiet part of the country, but we were very happy."

"It does not matter whether your house is big or small, if you are happy," the Marchioness said with a smile.

"That is what I realised when I was in Rome," Lorena said. "The girls used to talk about their stately homes, their Castles, and one or two even lived in Palaces. But I knew that however grand and important they were, I would give anything in the world merely to go home to my father and mother so that we could be together again."

"That was what was important?" the Marchioness asked.

"It was important because we were a family," Lorena explained. "Papa used to say to me that families were especially blessed because Jesus had chosen to have a father and mother and quite an ordinary home, until He started to preach."

"But supposing," the Marchioness said, "there had been no love in your home?"

"It is impossible to imagine that," Lorena answered, "because Mama loved Papa so deeply, and they loved me."

She paused for a moment, then said:

"Mama once said that it was the woman who makes a home and who gives it the love that encircles it with happiness."

"Your mother loved your father, so it was easy for her," the Marchioness murmured.

"Mama gave everybody love," Lorena said. "The people in the village adored her, and her friends all came to her when they were in trouble because she would help them. She said to me once:

" 'We may be poor, Lorena, but love is without price. It is more valuable than any other commodity in the world.' "

The Marchioness smiled at her.

"Thank you, dear child."

As she spoke, she rose to her feet.

Lorena had been so intent on what she was saying that she had not noticed that the Duke had joined the party and the Butler had announced luncheon.

Only as they went towards the Dining-Room did she realise with a sense of relief that the Countess of Hellingford was not present and there was another lady sitting beside the Duke at the head of the table.

She felt shy of looking at him because she was so vividly aware of his presence, and she did not meet his eyes until halfway through luncheon.

Then as if she could not help herself she found herself looking at him, and in that second his eyes held hers. She felt that they spoke without words and were both thinking of what had happened at dawn.

Then as the Marchioness spoke to him he turned his head, and as if she came back from a long way away Lorena realised that the man sitting next to her was waiting for her to reply to something he had said.

After what seemed a very drawn-out meal, the whole party moved automatically into the Blue Drawing-Room.

"As we have not made any plans for this afternoon," the Duke said, "I wondered if you would think it amusing to drive or ride over to the Folly. It is about five miles away and was built by one of my ancestors who had too much money and too little sense. We could have a picnic-tea there."

"That sounds delightful!" the Marchioness exclaimed.

"I am prepared to look at all the Follies, wherever they are built, providing I can race you on one of your horses, Alstone," Lord Carnforth ejaculated.

"That is what I would like too," Major Fane agreed.

"We might have a steeple-chase," someone else said. "I am sure Alstone could provide us with some enviable prizes."

"It is certainly an idea," the Duke said. "What about you, Perry?"

"I am prepared to race anyone and everyone," Perry replied, "as long as I can choose my horse."

"You can have any one in the stable as long as you do not choose mine," the Duke said.

"That is taking an unfair advantage!" one man exclaimed.

"Not really," the Duke replied, "because if I win, I promise not to take the first prize but to pass it on to whoever is second."

"Are we going to draw up some rules about this race, Alstone?" Archie Carnforth asked. "I think most of us know this part of the country anyway, and personally I think it would be most fun if it was a point-to-point from here to the Folly."

"You must let us go first," the Marchioness said, "because otherwise we will not be there in time to greet the victor."

"That is sensible," the Duke approved. "Now, who is going by carriage and who is going to ride?"

He looked towards Lorena as he spoke, and he knew by the light in her eyes that she wanted to ride.

"The ladies can ride if they wish," he said, "but they may not compete."

"Are you suggesting," asked the Viscountess of Storr, "that we are not capable of riding as well as the men?"

"You will certainly look far more attractive when you start," the Duke replied, "but as this is quite a hard ride, I dread to think of how you will appear by the end of it!"

"Do not be tiresome, Sarah," the Marchioness exclaimed. "I intend to ride, and we will leave half-an-hour before those who are going to race, so we will get there in comfort. It is far too hot to be energetic."

"I personally am going to drive," one of the ladies said positively, and two of the other women agreed that that was their preference also.

"Well, we ought to go and get ready," the Marchioness said. "Come along, Lorena. We can only hope we will not find that all the best horses have been taken before we come down again."

The Marchioness was already moving towards the door when the Countess of Hellingford appeared.

She had changed her gown and was wearing, to Lorena's surprise, a flat motoring-hat from which streamed a long chiffon veil.

Over one arm she carried a dust-coat such as ladies always wore when they were in an open car, and both her hands were beneath it as if it were a muff.

She swept imperiously down the room, stopped just before she reached Lorena and the Marchioness, and stood staring at the Duke, who detached himself from the men to whom he was talking.

"I have come to say good-bye, Alstone," the Countess said loudly, "to you and to your friends."

Everybody stopped talking and there was silence as she went on:

"You have made it very clear that you do not wish to have me here, and I certainly have no desire to stay where I am not wanted."

She paused for a moment and the Duke interposed:

"Please, Daisy . . ."

The Countess continued as if he had not spoken:

"I am going back to London, and I shall never, make no mistake, *never* set foot in this accursed place again! I loathe Mere and I loathe you, Alstone, for what you have done to me!"

She paused again. Then she said distinctly and with a venomous note in her voice that was un-mistakable:

"But make no mistake—if you will not make *me* happy, no other woman shall have what belongs to me!"

Before she said the last three words she had drawn her right hand from beneath the dust-coat, and Lorena saw with horror that she held a small revolver in her hand.

The Countess spoke the words "belongs to me" slowly, accentuating them as if she wished them to be particularly dramatic.

Then she pointed the pistol so that the bullet would hit the Duke below the waist.

But before she could pull the trigger, Lorena, driven by instinct that was swifter than thought, seized the Countess's arm and forced it upwards.

There was a resounding explosion as the bullet passed just above the Duke's shoulder, grazing the cloth of his coat, to bury itself in the mirror over the mantelpiece and smash the glass into a thou-sand pieces.

There was a scream but otherwise everyone else present was astounded into silence.

Then as Lorena released her grip, the Countess brought down the revolver with all her strength on the girl who had prevented her revenge from being effective.

It caught Lorena on the side of the temple and she fell to the ground as if poleaxed.

Then as Perry snatched the revolver from Daisy's hand, the Duke moved forward to kneel be-side Lorena.

Lorena was unconscious and was therefore quite unaware of the pandemonium that broke out.

Everybody was talking and exclaiming at once, while the Countess, her eyes flashing, a flush on her cheeks, merely stood staring at the Duke, who did not even raise his head to look at her.

"How could you do such a terrible thing?" Sir Hugo demanded angrily. "You might have killed Alstone, and you would have hanged for it!"

"It would not have killed him. I would merely have stopped his philandering, if your niece had not interfered!"

"You should be very grateful that she did so," Sir Hugo retorted. "Think of the scandal it would have caused if you had killed or injured Alstone. If anyone talks about what has happened here, the Press will get hold of it and that would be disastrous."

The rest of the members of the house-party were all standing, staring at Daisy as if they could not believe what they had seen.

The Duke, with Lorena in his arms, rose to his feet.

"Send for a Doctor," he said sharply to Perry, who happened to be standing closest to him.

Without saying another word he walked towards the door.

As he disappeared, a hubbub of voices broke out and Sir Hugo held up his hand.

"Now listen to me, all of you!" he said. "I want you to swear by everything you hold sacred that not one of you will mention what has just occurred to anyone outside this room."

The Countess made a derisive sound and made as if to leave, but Sir Hugo barred her way.

"You will swear too, Daisy," he said, "and make no mistake—I am not trying to save your reputation but my niece's."

"Your niece is not involved, except that she prevented me from treating Alstone as he deserves!" Daisy snapped.

"You know as well as I do that if it got about that she saved Alstone's life and that she was involved in a quarrel which concerned you and him, the child would be snubbed socially in a manner which would be most unfair and would do her a lot of harm."

He saw that the Countess was undecided, and he went on:

"If you do not agree to what I suggest, then I shall not only have no compunction in telling your husband the truth of this whole unsavoury affair, but I shall also make it my business to acquaint Their Majesties with the facts of the matter!"

The Countess looked at him in surprise. Then as she realised that she was defeated, she shrugged her shoulders.

"Very well then," she said, "I give you my promise, but I do not see why Alstone should get away scot-free."

Sir Hugo did not reply, he merely looked at the other members of the house-party and asked:

"Will you all give me your promise, without reservation, that nothing will be said about Daisy's behaviour or the very fortunate way in which Lorena saved our host from being killed or wounded?"

"I promise!"

Everybody in the party murmured the words simultaneously, and Sir Hugo said:

"Thank you. And now, Daisy, I suggest the sooner you go, the better!"

"I have every intention of leaving," the Countess replied with what dignity she could muster. "But I would like to speak to Alstone first."

"That is something I have no intention of allowing you to do," Sir Hugo said. "You have done enough damage for one day. Go back to London, Daisy, and thank your lucky stars that it is not a great deal worse than it is. You are a wicked woman and I hope I do not meet you again for a very long time."

The Countess tossed her head and walked from the room.

Sir Hugo watched her go, then drew his handkerchief from his breast-pocket and wiped his forehead.

"All I can say is thank God for Lorena!" Perry remarked. "Now I must get the Doctor, as Alstone told me to do."

"And I will go and see how she is," Sir Hugo said.

They left the room together, and the others who were left behind all began to talk at once.

Sir Hugo could hear their voices as he hurried up the stairs.

He found that the Duke had already laid Lorena down on her bed.

Her face was very pale and she looked young, frail, and vulnerable, and there was already a large angry red mark on the side of her temple where the revolver had struck her.

The Duke was standing by the bed, looking down at her, as Sir Hugo came to his side.

"I have not rung for the maid at the moment,"

the Duke said, "because I thought we first ought to decide what we should say both to the servants and of course to the Doctor."

"I have made everyone in the party swear that what has happened shall go no further," Sir Hugo said in a low voice.

"I thought you would do that," the Duke said. "Thank you, Hugo."

"I was thinking of Lorena, and I threatened Daisy that I will not only tell her husband but also the King and Queen if she breathes a word of what actually occurred."

"She must be out of her mind!" the Duke said in a low voice.

"I warned you a long time ago that she is uncontrolled, and also rotten to the core."

"You were right," the Duke said briefly.

Sir Hugo looked at Lorena.

"I think we should just say that the child slipped on the polished parquet and fell against one of the tables. It could have happened that way."

"I suppose so," the Duke agreed. "I will see that the servants hear that story, and you can tell the Doctor."

He moved towards the door and Sir Hugo said:

"If I were you, Alstone, I should leave the others to get over the shock. They were chattering like an aviary of parrots when I came up the stairs."

"I have every intention of going somewhere *alone*," the Duke said, accentuating the word.

"I think that is wise of you," Sir Hugo remarked, and put out his hand towards the bell-pull.

Chapter Seven

Kelvin Fane walked into the Library, where the Duke was at his desk writing.

"I am leaving now, Alstone."

The Duke looked up in surprise.

"So early, Kelvin? I was not expecting you to go until later."

"I want to get up to London early this afternoon," Major Fane replied, "because I have made a decision of which I think you will approve."

"What is that?" the Duke asked.

He rose from his desk and walked across the room to stand with his back to the fireplace.

"I have been thinking," Kelvin Fane said, as if he was choosing his words with care, "that there seems a likelihood that we shall be at war with Germany before we are very much older."

"Do you really think that a possibility?" the Duke enquired.

Kelvin Fane nodded.

"I was talking to the Commander-in-Chief last month, and he is convinced that we should be prepared, which we are certainly not at the moment."

"In which case, what do you intend to do about it?" the Duke asked.

"I am going to the War Office as soon as I ar-

rive in London, to apply to be posted to the Staff
College at Camberley for a course."

The Duke looked surprised and Kelvin Fane
said:

"It is what the Commander-in-Chief suggested
to me. He was really rather flattering. He said:
'You are one of the men, Fane, who, if there is
a war, I would like to have on my staff.' "

The Major paused for a moment before he
added:

"I laughed at the time, but now I have come to
the conclusion that it is time I did something a little more serious than waste my intelligence with
women like Sarah."

This was such plain speaking that the Duke was
astounded.

He had never known Kelvin Fane to talk to him
so frankly before on matters that were intimate
and private.

He was silent for a moment, then he said:

"Has this sudden decision on your part anything
to do with what occurred on Monday?"

"Of course it has!" Kelvin Fane replied. "But
even before Daisy behaved in such an outrageous
manner, it was Lorena, actually, who made me realise that I was wasting my life."

The Duke raised his eye-brows as he asked:

"Is your interest in Lorena serious?"

"Shall I say that I am thinking about her seriously," Kelvin Fane replied, "and I intend to see
her as soon as she leaves here. After that, I may
be able to answer you more positively."

When he had finished speaking, he held out his
hand.

"Good-bye, Alstone, and thank you for a very

unusual visit to Mere! I cannot think of any other way to describe it."

The Duke took his hand and said:

"I will come and see you off."

"No, stay where you are," Kelvin Fane replied. "I can see that you are busy."

"I am writing a speech which I want to make in the House of Lords," the Duke said. "It has been on my conscience for some time, but I have been too lazy to set it down in writing."

"We all seem to have been activated out of our indolence these last few days," Kelvin Fane remarked.

He walked towards the door, and as he reached it he turned back to say:

"I have paid my debt to Hugo. I consider that he won the contest hands down! And by the way, Lionel Dartford is waiting to see you. Shall I send him in?"

"Yes, of course," the Duke replied.

When he was alone he did not go back to his writing-desk. Instead, he stood looking across the great Library with a very thoughtful expression in his eyes.

Only a few minutes passed before the door opened and Lord Dartford came into the room.

"Like Fane, I only want to say good-bye," he said, "and of course to thank you for your hospitality."

"I wanted to see you anyway," the Duke replied, "but everybody is leaving earlier than I expected."

Lord Dartford grinned.

"I think the truth is that they are feeling a little embarrassed."

"Which is not surprising," the Duke said drily.

Lord Dartford held out his hand.

"Well, good-bye, then."

"No, wait a minute," the Duke said. "I have something to suggest to you which I think you might find interesting."

"What is that?"

"I had a letter a week ago from the Maharajah of Cochapour. He asked me if I could recommend anybody completely honest and trustworthy, in this country, who could buy him a large number of polo-ponies for his team."

"One of the best in India," Lord Dartford murmured.

"And who would also purchase on his behalf," the Duke continued, "a great quantity of furnishings which he needs for a new Palace he is building."

The Duke smiled as he continued:

"You can imagine what they will be—very expensive chandeliers, gold-framed mirrors, and of course superlative carpets, all of which will be extremely expensive."

Lord Dartford was listening to the Duke with rapt attention but he did not say anything, and the Duke went on:

"The Maharajah, who, as you are aware, is one of the richest men in India, suggested that whoever undertakes to serve him in this way would be entitled not only to a salary and expenses but also to a large commission on everything that is purchased."

The Duke paused before he added:

"I can think of no-one more qualified to fill the position than you, Lionel."

Lord Dartford drew in a deep breath.

"Do you really mean that, Alstone? It is something I would very much enjoy doing, besides the fact that I have made such a fool of myself not only over the money I have lost here, but in buying a number of dud shares. Actually I am in 'Queer Street.' "

"Then this will get you out of it," the Duke said. "As it happens, I had anticipated that you would accept my suggestion, and I have already written to the Maharajah and put forward your name. I told him I would trust your judgement on horseflesh anywhere and that in furnishing his Palace your taste would be as good as mine!"

Lord Dartford made an inarticulate little sound and the Duke went on quickly:

"Before you leave, look in my secretary's office and read the letter in case there are any amendments you would like to make."

"I do not know how to thank you..." Lord Dartford began in a hoarse voice.

"I shall be very embarrassed if you try," the Duke said. "I think really we should be thanking Lorena. It was she who brought to my notice the fact that the stakes played in this house were far too high. This is something which will not happen in the future."

"She is the pluckiest girl I have ever known in my whole life!" Lord Dartford exclaimed. "Will you tell her so when she is better? Also tell Hugo, if I do not see him, that he has been proved right so indisputably over the 'Pygmalion' contest that Archie will have to pay up and like it!"

"He certainly will," the Duke agreed, "and I will see that he does!"

There were more expressions of gratitude on Lord Dartford's part before the two men parted.

The Duke returned to his desk, and had been writing for some time when the Marchioness of Trumpington, looking extremely attractive in a motoring-hat with clouds of blue chiffon trailing from it, peeped round the door.

"Are you alone, Alstone?" she enquired.

"Enid!" the Duke exclaimed. "I had no idea it was so late! I knew that you and Jack were leaving at three o'clock and I meant to be waiting for you."

"It is not yet three and Jack is fussing about the car," the Marchioness replied, "but I wanted to speak to you."

"Of course!" the Duke said. "Come and sit down."

The Marchioness seated herself on the sofa, looked up at the Duke, and smiled.

"I can see you are apprehensive," she said, "but you will be pleased at what I have to tell you."

"I hope so."

"I think you may have anticipated that I might say that Jack and I were going to do something desperate like running away together," the Marchioness said.

"It had crossed my mind," the Duke admitted. "Something that Jack said, the first night you were here, made me wonder what I could do to stop you."

"There is no need for you to do anything," the Marchioness answered. "What I have come to tell you, Alstone, is that we had intended to leave England, Jack and I. In fact, we came to Mere be-

cause we thought it would be a good opportunity
to be together and finalise our plans."

"Now you have changed your minds?" the Duke
asked, with a note of relief in his voice.

"It was Lorena who did that," the Marchioness
said quietly.

"Lorena?" the Duke exclaimed incredulously.

"She is so young and innocent, and yet she has
about her a kind of aura which I can only describe
as one of goodness."

The Marchioness gave a little sigh.

"It made me remember what I was like at her
age, idealistic, romantic, believing the world was a
wonderful place and that if I was happy I would
make everybody else happy too."

The Marchioness paused. The Duke did not
speak, and after a moment she went on:

"When I looked at her and listened to her, I
knew that what Jack and I contemplated would
not only hurt my husband, who in his own way has
shown me nothing but kindness, but would also
damage a great number of other people, simply because they are our friends."

She looked round the Library as if she were seeing it for the first time; then she said:

"Mere and other houses like it, people like yourself, Alstone, and of course the Trumpington family, in the public's mind stand not only for the
grandeur of this country but for its stability."

Her voice deepened as she continued:

"I have begun to understand that the obligations
I owe to my position in the Social World are in a
way more important than the dictates of my heart,
and that also applies to Jack."

The Marchioness made a very expressive little gesture with her hands before she said:

"I love him! I love him desperately, and he loves me, but he has a position of importance in his own County, the people he employs on his Estate respect him, and his children love him and he loves them."

Her voice trembled for a moment, then she added:

"We will go on seeing each other discreetly, and perhaps one day—who knows? Fate may be kind to us. Until then, we will play the parts we have to play, and I hope we do so with dignity."

The Duke sat down beside the Marchioness and took her hand in his.

"Thank you for telling me this, Enid," he said. "I admire both you and Jack for coming to such a decision, which I know is the right one."

"I am sure it is," the Marchioness replied. "And please tell that sweet child that as soon as she is well enough I want her to come and stay with me. If Kitty will not chaperone her I will do so myself, and it is something I would greatly enjoy."

"I will tell Lorena."

"And thank you, Alstone dear," the Marchioness said, "for being the most wonderful friend Jack and I ever had. I know that if anyone will help us in the years that lie ahead, it will be you."

"You may be sure of that," the Duke replied.

He kissed the Marchioness's hand, and when they both rose to their feet, she bent forward and kissed him on the cheek.

"Thank you, Alstone," she said again, and there were tears in her eyes.

The Duke walked with her to the Hall, found

that Lord Gilmour was waiting beside the car at the front door, and saw them off on their journey to London.

He thought as he walked back up the steps into the house that he might have felt very differently had they been driving in the opposite direction, setting off for the Continent.

The Marchioness was right—their positions carried responsibilities which neither of them could ignore.

The Duke was walking across the Hall when Sir Hugo came down the staircase.

"Has Enid gone?" he asked. "I wanted to say good-bye to her."

"She has just left."

"Well, I shall see them in London."

"Yes, in London."

Sir Hugo reached the Hall and the Duke asked:

"How is Lorena? Has the Doctor seen her?"

"Yes, he was here about an hour ago," Sir Hugo replied. "She will be able to get up tomorrow. He does not wish her to travel until Thursday, if that is all right with you."

"Of course it is!" the Duke replied. "And I would rather like to talk to her now, if that is possible."

"I have just moved her into the *Boudoir* next to her bedroom," Sir Hugo replied; "she is to have tea there."

"Then I will go and talk to her," the Duke said. "I have various messages to give her from the guests who have already left, and Enid has suggested that she should go and stay with her, if Kitty does not want her."

As he spoke, he glanced at Sir Hugo and saw his lips tighten in a hard line.

"Have you and Kitty made any decision about Lorena's future?" he asked.

"In this instance it will be a question of what *I* want!" Sir Hugo replied.

The Duke's eyes twinkled but he did not say anything.

Sir Hugo, as if he was anxious to change the subject, said:

"By the way, you will be amused to hear that Archie paid up like a sportsman before he left this morning. He said he could hardly argue with someone who had made a Grand Slam!"

Sir Hugo gave a little laugh.

"What was more, Archie had no wish to argue, because he was in such a hurry to get to London. I would not mind betting that his real reason is that he wants to get to the Club before Kelvin or Jack to expound *his* contention that different kinds of water affect the running of a horse!"

The Duke laughed.

"I am sure Archie will take all the credit for that idea, even though we all know it was Lorena's."

"She has certainly done me proud!" Sir Hugo said. "I do not mind telling you now that as I waited at Victoria Station I was very nervous as to what she would be like. But she not only 'turned up trumps,' but, as Archie put it, she made a Grand Slam as well!"

"Will it be all right if I go up to see her now?" the Duke asked.

Sir Hugo had the idea that his host had not been listening to what he had been saying, so he merely replied:

"Yes, of course. She has a nasty bruise on her temple, but otherwise I do not think there is much wrong."

He realised, however, that he was talking to thin air, for the Duke had left and was already climbing the stairs.

*　*　*

Lorena, sitting on the *chaise-longue* in the *Boudoir* that was attached to her bedroom, was wondering which of the books that Mrs. Kingston had put beside her would be best to read.

Her uncle had already told her they could leave for London on Thursday, and she felt, almost childishly, that when there was so much at Mere she had to leave behind, it would add to her feeling of regret if she also left a half-finished novel.

Lying back against the silk cushions with a lace and satin cover over her legs, she looked round the room as if it was another item to store in her memory.

The cupids in the Boucher paintings on the walls echoed those painted on the ceiling, the exquisite pieces of French furniture, and the turquoise blue of the curtains and coverings on the Louis XIV chairs were all photographed in her mind.

"Everything at Mere is so lovely!" she told herself.

However, because she must leave it, there was a pain in her breast far more intense than the ache in her temple.

Yet if she was honest, it was the owner of Mere who would haunt her for the rest of her life, and would be not only in her mind but in her heart and soul for all eternity.

'I saved him!' she had thought with an irrepressible elation when she had recovered consciousness.

Although her head had ached almost unbearably and she felt a little sick and shaken by what had occurred, nothing mattered except that the Duke was uninjured and she had been able to prevent the Countess from hurting him as she had tried to do.

"How could any woman be so ... cruel ... so wicked?" Lorena asked herself.

She knew that because she loved the Duke she wanted to protect him not only from anything that would hurt him spiritually but also from unhappiness and disillusionment.

If he loved the Countess it would have been terrible for him to watch her behaving in such a manner; but if, as it appeared from what she had said, he no longer loved her, then surely there must have been the humiliation of knowing that he had wasted his love on someone who could behave in such an unrestrained, vulgar manner.

'I saved him ... then,' Lorena thought, 'but ... suppose she tries ... again?'

It was an inexpressible agony to think that the Duke might again be in danger and she would not be there to protect him.

Then she told herself that she was being ridiculous.

She could never mean anything in the Duke's life. She had been extremely fortunate in being able to express her love in a manner that she had never dreamt of.

It was just chance that she had been in that particular place at that particular moment.

Had she been standing anywhere else in the

room, however strong her instinct of danger might
have been, she would have been too late to deflect
the bullet from where it was intended.

"You were very brave, and I was very proud
of you!" Sir Hugo had said when he came to see
her last night after the Doctor had gone.

Lorena had longed to ask him what the Duke
had said and what he had thought, but she had
been too shy and had found it difficult to say anything.

Because Sir Hugo had thought she was sleepy
and should be left to rest as quietly as possible, he
had gone away and she had been alone with her
thoughts.

Now she knew that if she opened one of the
books which lay at her side, she would find it difficult to concentrate on the pages. All she would
see would be the Duke's face.

Because it made her happy and was far more
enthralling than anything she could read, she lay
back and started to think over all that had happened from the first moment she had met him.

There was that morning when they had gone
riding together, then had breakfast alone in the
ancient farm-house.

'That is what I want to do again,' Lorena
thought.

But she was asking for the impossible, and once
she left Mere, the Duke would be as inaccessible
as the moon.

She shut her eyes as if it would minimise the
pain which she knew she would feel when they
said good-bye.

Then there was a knock on the door, and before
she could answer, the Duke came into the room.

For a moment, because she was thinking of him so intensely, she could hardly realise that he was actual and not a part of her imagination.

But as he walked towards the *chaise-longue* on which she was lying, she felt the blood rising in her cheeks because of the look in his eyes and because her hair was falling over her shoulders and she was wearing only her dressing-gown under the satin and lace cover.

It was a very demure garment that she had worn at the Convent, of white crêpe, plainly cut and buttoned down the front, with a flat collar at the neck and long sleeves.

It made Lorena look, especially with her hair down, very young and at the same time almost ethereal, as if she were not human but one of the classical statues that the Duke had thought her to be when he had seen her standing in the darkness on the roof.

He reached the *chaise-longue* and held out his hand.

"How are you, Lorena?" he asked. "Your uncle said you were well enough to see me."

"I am . . . quite well," Lorena replied in a voice that did not sound like her own. "Tomorrow I can . . . get up."

Because he was expecting it, she put out her hand and he held it in both of his. Then to her surprise he sat down beside her on the edge of the *chaise-longue,* rather than in a chair, as she would have expected.

"You are very lovely," he said, "and I always thought your hair would look as it does now."

Lorena's cheeks were crimson and her eyes flick-

ered, and as she looked down, her eye-lashes were
dark against her skin.

He still kept her hand in his and after a moment
he said:

"I must start, before we say all the things we
have to tell each other, by thanking you for saving
my life."

He felt her fingers quiver and knew it was because she was afraid of what might have happened
to him.

Then he went on:

"I want you to try to forget what happened. It
was ugly and unpleasant, and it is not the sort of
thing I want you ever to think about again."

"I . . . I was . . . afraid for . . . you."

"I know," the Duke replied, "and it was very
perceptive and clever of you to have anticipated
what might happen. But I am safe, so do not think
of it any more."

There was a note of authority in his voice, and
Lorena replied:

"I will . . . try."

"There are a great number of other things to
think about," the Duke said with a smile, "but first
of all, I have a message for you from the Marchioness. She would like you to go and stay with
her not only on a visit but, if you wish, indefi-
nitely."

Lorena looked at him in surprise.

"You mean . . . I could live . . . with her?"

"That, I think, is what she would like, but I believe your uncle has other ideas."

"Uncle Hugo did say . . . something which made
me think he . . . might want me . . . but I have a
feeling that Aunt Kitty will . . . send me away."

"At least you have two propositions to consider," the Duke said, "and I have a third."

Lorena looked at him but did not speak, and he thought it would be impossible for any other woman's eyes to be more revealing.

He looked down at the hand he still held in his, then said as if he was choosing his words carefully:

"I expect you will remember, because you are well-read, that the Greeks always said that if you saved a man's life, he was your responsibility forever."

There was silence and Lorena's fingers were tense as the Duke continued quietly:

"I am wondering, therefore, Lorena, what you intend to do about me."

"I . . . I do not . . . understand."

"I think you should look after me," the Duke said, "for I need you as I have never needed anyone else."

He knew by the way her fingers quivered that a vague understanding of what he was saying had come to her mind. At the same time, she dared not accept it.

"What . . . are you asking me to . . . do?" she enquired in a voice he could barely hear.

"I am asking you to marry me, my darling," the Duke said. "I knew I loved you when we watched the dawn together, but I have had no chance of telling you so until now."

"Y-you . . . love . . . me?"

The words held a joy that was almost untranslatable into sound.

"I love you!" the Duke said. "And I think, perhaps because already our minds are so close to each other, you love me a little."

"I love you! Of course I love you!" Lorena said. "I love you until it is a glory that fills the sky ... but I cannot ... marry ... you."

The words were almost inaudible, but the Duke heard them.

"Did you say you would not marry me?" he asked incredulously.

It had never occurred to him that a woman, any woman, would refuse him if he offered her marriage, and least of all Lorena.

"I cannot ... marry you," Lorena said, and now her voice was firm, "but I shall always be . . . inexpressibly proud that you ... asked me."

The Duke's fingers tightened on hers.

"Why will you not marry me?" he asked. "You said you love me."

"I do love you, and it is the most ... wonderful thing imaginable that ... you should love me too ... but I am not the ... right wife for you ... as I would not be able to make you ... happy."

"You are thinking of me?" the Duke asked.

"Of course I am ... thinking of ... you."

There was a faint smile on the Duke's lips as she went on:

"When I knew I ... loved you ... I never dreamt ... never imagined for one second that you would ever ... love me ... and although it is an ... agony to think of leaving you ..."

Her voice broke on the words, but then she went on:

"I know my memories of you will ... always be in my heart ... and will help me when I can no longer ... see you and no longer ... hear your voice."

"You feel like that, and yet you will not marry me?"

"It is ... because I love you ... so much."

Her voice trembled as she continued:

"I was thinking just now before you came into the room that ... because I love you I want to ... protect you ... to take care of you ... and prevent anyone else from ... injuring you not only physically ... but by hurting your ... mind ... or your feelings."

She drew a deep breath before she said:

"That is what I should want to do ... if I ... married you."

"But you are refusing me?"

"Because I could not take ... part in your life ... or be ... accepted by your friends."

She looked up at him, wanting him to understand.

"I am not only ... ignorant ... but foolish where they are ... concerned ... and ... "

She stopped.

"And?" the Duke prompted.

Lorena did not speak, and he asked very gently:

"Tell me what else you feel."

She glanced up at him and her words came with a rush:

"I am ... shocked at the way they ... behave!"

Now it was impossible for her to look at the Duke, and because she thought he would be angry, she held on to his hand tightly as she had held it before when they had watched the dawn.

The Duke understood everything she was trying

to say, and the expression on his face was one which no woman had ever seen before.

"So to save me from being unhappy," he said, "you are prepared to go away and leave me, knowing our love for each other is something so unique, so overwhelming, that to me it is like the sun we saw filling the sky with its fire and beauty."

"Is it . . . really like . . . that to you?" Lorena whispered.

"All that and very much more," the Duke replied. "And as you and I saw the sun sweep away the night, so our love will sweep from our lives all that is dark and ugly, and everything, my darling, that shocks you."

"Supposing . . . supposing you become . . . unhappy because you . . . married me?"

"If you will not marry me I shall be so abjectly miserable that I shall think life is not worth living."

She made a little sound of joy and the Duke went on:

"But if you are worried, my precious one, about not being accepted by my friends, I have something to tell you."

"What is . . . that?" Lorena asked.

"The reason why your uncle brought you to Mere," the Duke said, "was that he and Lord Carnforth had an argument over a play called *Pygmalion*. Have you read it?"

"Yes, I read it while I was here," Lorena answered. "I found the book in your Library."

"I intend to read it myself, but I have not yet had time," the Duke said. "But you, having read it, will understand that the argument arose because Lord Carnforth said that what the Professor had done in transforming a girl—I think her name was Eliza Doolittle—so that she was accepted in Society was completely impossible."

Lorena's eyes were wide with interest as he went on:

"Your uncle, on the other hand, said it was perfectly credible. There was a wordy duel between the two, with all the men present taking sides. Then Lord Carnforth demanded that your uncle should prove his point by bringing a young girl to Mere who would be accepted at the end of her visit as one of the Windlemere Set."

"And that was . . . I?" Lorena asked in amazement.

"Your uncle had no idea of what you would be like," the Duke replied, "but because he and Archie Carnforth are often at loggerheads with each other, he agreed to the competition."

"That first night," Lorena murmured, "when everybody looked at me in a . . . curious manner, I had a feeling there was something I did not . . . understand."

"You charmed us all," the Duke said, "and when we had breakfast together the next morning, when I knew you were not in the least what I expected, in fact I felt nervous because you intrigued me so much."

"Nervous?" Lorena questioned.

"Shall I say you enchanted me?" the Duke said. "I knew I was falling in love."

His face drew a little nearer to hers as he went on:

"I felt as I had never felt before, not only a desire to touch you and kiss you because you were so lovely, but I also wanted to protect you, to look after you, and keep you safe from anything that might harm you."

"That . . . is what I . . . felt about you."

"I think love, real love, arouses everybody in the same way," the Duke said.

He bent nearer still as he said very softly:

"How can I deny what is the most wonderful thing in the world, a love which tells me you are the woman I have been looking for all my life?"

"And you are the . . . Prince Charming I have . . . dreamt about."

Lorena was not able to say any more, for the Duke's lips were on hers and his arms were round her.

He held her very close and thought that no other woman could be more soft, more sweet, and more pure and good.

Then as he felt an almost incredible rapture rise within him, which was very different from anything he had ever known before, he knew, as Lorena did, that it was an ecstasy which came from God.

What she felt for the Duke was like the sun sweeping over the horizon, blinding and glorious, its rays shooting up into the sky so that the stars faded before its glory.

She felt as if the Duke took her heart and soul from between her lips and made them his, and she thought too that the strength of his arms gave her a security that she had not felt since her father and mother had died.

But now she was his and never again would she feel lonely and afraid.

The Duke raised his head to look down at her,

and because she was so happy her eyes were full of sunshine as she murmured:

"I ... love ... you ... I love ... you!"

She was whispering the words which she had said a thousand times during the night but never thought she could say to him.

"I love you too!" the Duke said. "Oh, my precious, my darling, what would have happened to me *if* I had never met you? *If* Shaw had never written *Pygmalion,* and *if* your uncle and Archie Carnforth had not argued about it?"

"Perhaps it was ... fate that I ... to Mere," Lorena said, "but I think fate would have ... brought us together anyway."

She gave him an entrancing little smile as she said:

"I might have saved you from being run over by a motor-car, or run down by an express train!"

The Duke laughed.

"You have a lifetime to prevent any such things from happening to me, and I will protect you, my lovely one, from anything that might shock you, and that is a vow!"

"B-but ... I cannot ask you to ... change your ... whole life."

"You will not only change my life," the Duke said, "but I know, because you are you and because, as you told me, the life-force that you give out is a power for good, that you will change the lives of those who matter to us as friends. The others are of no account."

As he spoke, he thought of how Lorena had already altered the life of the Marchioness of Trumpington and that of Jack Gilmour; how Kelvin Fane would now have something to occupy his mind other than "flitting from *Boudoir* to *Boudoir*"; and how Sir Hugo had unexpectedly found a new determination which might prevent his wife from behaving so badly in the future.

It was extraordinary what one small person could do just because she had the right ideas, and perhaps, as she herself believed, she was helped by a power given her by God.

"Are you . . . sure . . . quite sure," Lorena asked, "that it would be . . . right for you to . . . marry me?"

"It would be everything that was wrong *not to* marry you!" the Duke replied. "But rightly or wrongly, I have every intention of making you my wife, and nothing and no-one shall stop me!"

He spoke with a determination which made Lorena look at him admiringly.

"I love you . . . when you are like . . . that."

"Like what?" he asked.

"Strong and authoritative. I thought at first it was rather . . . overwhelming . . . but it is how you should be. A leader . . . someone whom everyone looks up to and admires."

"You will make me conceited!" The Duke smiled. "But I know, my darling, that I can be none of those things unless you are with me to show me how."

"That is . . . what I want," Lorena said, "but . . . "

"No 'buts'!" the Duke interrupted. "You want me to be authoritative and that is what I am! I intend to make you my wife as quickly as possible so that we can be together for always! Then we will teach each other about our love. As far as I am concerned, I think there is a great deal for me to learn."

He did not allow Lorena to answer.

His lips were on hers and he was kissing her demandingly, insistently, and a little more fiercely than he had done before, as if he wished to make sure of her and allay some lingering fear within him that she might at the last moment escape him.

It seemed to Lorena as if the sun as it had come burningly and crimson over the horizon was now on his lips and in his eyes.

Also, because he demanded it of her, she wanted to be closer and still closer to him, until she became an integral part of his body, his mind, and his soul, as he was part of hers.

She knew that this was love as it should be, as her father had described it so often, and what she had always prayed she might find one day.

It would not have mattered, she knew, if the man she loved had been a Duke or a pauper, and although she found Mere wonderful, it was the Duke who had filled her whole existence until in the midst of all his treasures she could see only him.

The Duke kissed her until she felt as if she had left the world behind and he had lifted her from the roof of Mere up into the sky, and they were together in the heart of the sun.

"I love you! God, how I love you!" he said at length, his voice hoarse and unsteady. "When will vou marry me, my darling? I cannot wait to be sure of you, and to have you with me both by day and by night!"

"I am ... ready to marry you now ... at once!" Lorena replied.

He laughed.

"That is exactly what I wanted you to say, but I need to have a little time to arrange the wedding and also, I presume, to ask your uncle's permission."

He saw the expression on Lorena's face and asked:

"What is worrying you?"

"You may think it ... foolish of me," she said, "but I am afraid that if we have a ... big wedding with all your friends there, it will spoil what I ... feel for you and what you ... feel for me."

A little while ago, the Duke thought, he would not have understood what she was saying, but now he knew that the love he felt for Lorena was so precious, so sacred, and its beauty was as fragile as the petal of a flower, that nothing which was material or mundane must encroach upon it.

"When I ... marry you," Lorena was saying in a very soft voice, "I want the Church to be filled with God and His love ... not with ... people."

"That is what you shall have, my precious," the Duke said. "We will be married the day after to-morrow, in the Church where we prayed together on Sunday. Will that please you?"

"It would be wonderful!" Lorena exclaimed. "But ... suppose Uncle Hugo does not ... agree?"

"He will agree!" the Duke said positively. "And there will be no need for you to go back to London on Thursday. I will arrange for a Special Licence, and we need tell no-one what we are doing until it is all over and you are mine."

Lorena knew that although it was cowardly of her, she could not bear that Daisy Hellingford should have the chance of making a scene if she learnt that they were to be married.

She did not want the Duke's men-friends, in their joking manner, laughing and talking about them.

But most of all, she did not want women like the Viscountess of Storr and perhaps her aunt treating marriage as if it were something light and unimportant, and not a sacrament of love, which her father had said it should be.

The Duke was watching the expression in her eyes, and he said:

"Leave everything to me, my lovely one. I know what you are thinking, and I feel the same. We will be married with only your uncle to give you away. Then I will take you for our honeymoon to a house I own by the sea, where we will be completely alone and can think only of ourselves."

Lorena gave a little cry of sheer delight. Then she said:

"How can you be so wonderful? How can you understand all the things I want ... and still be ... you?"

"I understand you as you understand me," the Duke said. "That is because we belong to each other and have done so for many centuries of time."

"That is what I feel," Lorena said with an ecstatic little sigh. "And I am so happy, so wildly, crazily happy!"

She looked up at him, then said:

"Mr. Gillingham described this as a Fairy-Palace when I first saw it. Are you quite certain it is real, and I will not suddenly wake to find that this has all been a dream and you are, as you always have been, just the Prince Charming in my imagination?"

"I think if I am in your dreams," the Duke said, "you would be with me."

"I would want to be," Lorena said, "but I do want to believe that you will really be my husband and I your wife."

"You can be sure of that," the Duke replied. "I knew, my darling, when you slipped your hand into mine as we stood on the roof, that I would never lose you, never let you go."

His lips were seeking hers again, kissing her fiercely and passionately. It did not make her afraid, it only aroused her in a way which she did not understand.

She felt as if his lips were awakening a strange fire which was seeping in flickering flames through her body, sweeping away her fears until they receded into an oblivion from which they would never return.

She put her arms round the Duke's neck and drew him closer still.

Everywhere there was light—the light of love. The Duke's lips became more insistent as her arms tightened round him.

"I love you! I love you . . . and you . . . are carrying me up into the sky," she murmured, "until in the whole world and in . . . the Universe there is nothing but . . . you!"

He looked down at her and he thought the happiness in her face made him feel as if he too was lifted into the sky by the Divine power of love.

"I worship you, my precious," he said. "God has given you to me, and now you will be mine through all eternity."

It was a vow which came from his very soul, and as Lorena surrendered her lips to his again, she knew that this was the reality from which they would never awaken.

About the Author

Barbara Cartland, the celebrated romantic novelist, historian, playwright, lecturer, political speaker, and television personality, has now written well over two hundred-fifty books as well as recently recording an album of love songs with the London Philharmonic Orchestra. In private life she is a Dame of Grace of St. John of Jerusalem, has fought for better conditions and salaries for midwives, has championed the cause of old people, and has founded the first Romany Gypsy Camp in the world. Barbara Cartland is deeply interested in Vitamin Therapy and is President of the British National Association for Health.